Read
Across America

Exploring 7 U.S. Regions Through Popular Children's Literature

GLORIA ROTHSTEIN

SCHOLASTIC
PROFESSIONAL BOOKS

New York • Toronto • London • Sydney • Auckland

1

MAR 1999

Dedication

To my Mom... the travel expert.
And, to my sons, Hale and Ryan...
who always keep me going in the right direction.

With love...

Acknowledgments

I'd like to thank Terry Cooper, Helen Moore Sorvillo, Virginia Dooley, Shawn Richardson, and Vincent Ceci for adding their special touches to this project. I'd also like to thank Carol Mears, my favorite educator/resource person, for sharing her expertise with me. A note of thanks to the staff at the Boca Raton Library, and the many other professionals who contributed to the development of this book.

To my sons, Ryan and Hale, my Mom, my family, and friends—thanks for your love and support. Plus, a special thanks to Jodi, Andi, and Mickey... for always being there.

Cover design by Vincent Ceci and Jaime Lucero
Cover illustration by Therese Anderko
Interior design by Vincent Ceci and Frank Maiocco
Interior illustrations by Therese Anderko

ISBN # 0-590-60341-8
Copyright © 1995 by Gloria Rothstein
All rights reserved.
Printed in the U.S.A.

12 11 10 9 8 7 6 5 4 3 2 1   1 2 3 4 5 6 / 9

Table of Contents

Geographic Concepts & Skills Matrix

TITLE	AUTHOR	Identifying Regions	Noting Geographic Features	Identifying /Natural Resources	Appreciating People as Resources	Developing Respect for Environment	Noting the Effects of Weather and Climate	Identifying Native Animals	Learning about Transportation	Reading/Using Maps	Using a Globe	Using Direction Words/Tracing a Route	Identifying Native Plants	Recognizing Change
Make Way for Ducklings	Robert McCloskey		✔					✔		✔		✔		
Miss Rumphius	Barbara Cooney		✔		✔	✔							✔	✔
Owl Moon	Jane Yolen		✔			✔	✔	✔						
Three Days on a River in a Red Canoe	Vera B. Williams		✔			✔		✔	✔	✔		✔		
If You Want to Find Golden	Eileen Spinelli		✔		✔					✔		✔		
Tar Beach	Faith Ringgold		✔		✔		✔		✔					
Round Trip	Anne Jonas		✔	✔		✔	✔		✔			✔		
The Relatives Came	Cynthia Rylant		✔			✔			✔			✔		
Appalachia	Cynthia Rylant		✔	✔		✔								
Story of the White House	Kate Waters		✔	✔						✔		✔		✔
Georgia Music	Helen Griffith				✔	✔	✔		✔			✔		✔
Bigmama's	Donald Crews		✔	✔	✔				✔					
In the Tall, Tall Grass	Denise Fleming		✔		✔	✔	✔	✔						
Mole's Hill	Lois Ehlert		✔		✔	✔		✔					✔	
Thunder Cake	Patricia Polacco			✔		✔								
In Coal Country	Judith Hendershot		✔	✔					✔					
Roxaboxen	Alice McLerran		✔		✔	✔		✔					✔	
The House I Live In	Isadora Seltzer	✔	✔	✔	✔	✔	✔		✔			✔		✔
Legend of the Indian Paintbrush	Tomie dePaola		✔	✔	✔	✔						✔	✔	✔
All the Places to Love	Patricia MacLachlan		✔	✔									✔	✔
Alaska's Three Bears	Shelley Gill		✔				✔	✔		✔	✔	✔		✔
Anno's Journey	Mistsumasa Anno		✔			✔			✔			✔	✔	

Introduction

While working in the Beacon Hill section of Boston, Robert McCloskey noticed the ducks in the Boston Public Garden. That's how the idea for the children's classic *Make Way for Ducklings* originated. Thanks to this author, people of all ages can follow the ducks around that memorable setting... and enjoy a scenic tour of the area.

With this in mind, I realized that I could take kids on a cross-country tour. All I needed... were some good books. Wouldn't it be fun to "read across America" and travel from region to region? By focusing on special places, memorable settings, and important journeys, I could give children an interesting view of this country. My spirit of adventure and playful "Oh, the Places We Will Go," ideas would enable youngsters to take off in many different directions. From secret places... to hiding places... to meeting places... to spooky places... to cities and states around this country, just think, I told myself, how much children could learn and discover.

Share Books

Launch this project by reading aloud all kinds of books with interesting settings. Enjoy the books that I suggest... and add some of your own favorites. Appreciate the fact that the artwork and the descriptions can provide colorful pictures of familiar places... and take children to places they've never seen. Refer to maps and globes. Bring in travel brochures and pamphlets. Set up book displays. Turn reading into a hands-on adventure.

Behind The Scenes

Use the background information provided in this section to introduce the read-aloud, or to spark interest in that story setting. Make the book more enjoyable by sharing interesting facts about that place, the state, or the region of the country, where the

story is set. Explain the connection between the author and the setting or the illustrator and the place. Help youngsters discover that writers write about places they know. Note the importance of the setting, and the way visual images add to the story. Make children more aware of the sights, the sounds, and the smells in a variety of settings—including their own neighborhoods and surroundings.

Many Different Directions

Use the theme-related ideas in this section to enable students to take off in many different directions. Learn about history, geography, sociology, science, math, music, art, etc. Plan discussions, group activities, independent study, ongoing projects, and hands-on learning. Try all of the cross-curricular suggestions and activities or just a few. Let students' interests and abilities be your guide. Create an environment where youngsters get involved in the learning process and are eager to explore new avenues.

Activity Pages

Most of the books on this "cross country tour" can be enjoyed by children of all ages. Plus, additional book titles for each region can be found on page 112. The same is true for the related activity pages. Children should enjoy making observations... comparing places... creating new settings... drawing conclusions... offering their own points of view... experimenting with ideas... and sharing books and settings with friends and family.

A Word About Interactive Charts

Some activity pages suggest making interactive charts. These are large teacher-created individual charts with whole sentences or words written on separate strips of paper and placed in clear pockets. Children can be asked to replace one or more of the words in a chart to create new meanings rhymes, etc. For more on interactive charts read *Building Literacy with Interactive Charts* by Kristin Schlosser and Vicki Phillips (Scholastic Professional Books 1993).

Parent Connection

Make family members aware of this "Read Across America" project and encourage them to participate. The parent letter on page 7 provides details on what you are doing and how they can help. Send home a copy of the letter, so that you know by their responses how many parents would like to visit the classroom to share travel experiences, volunteer to read, etc. You might also ask parents to come to class to help with specific projects, or to prepare foods from different regions of the country. No matter where you begin this "sight-seeing" adventure, it will be easy to take off in many different directions. Study maps. Make maps. Guide youngsters through all kinds of settings. Point out scenery, wildlife, bridges, tunnels, skyscrapers, museums, landmarks, lighthouses, and natural wonders. Celebrate the beauty and diversity of our country. And enjoy the fact that books can take you and your students anywhere!

Dear Parent or Caregiver,

Our class will be going on a special journey... with books. By sharing a variety of stories and selections, we will take a cross-country tour.

As we "read across America," we plan to meet many popular authors and discover some memorable settings. Hopefully, our books will take us to different states... different regions... and to places of interest all over the country.

Perhaps you could add something to the "sight-seeing" part of our trip.

We'd love you to share your own views of a visit to...

❑ Washington, D. C.

❑ a national park

❑ a historical place

❑ a well-known landmark

❑ another part of the country

❑ a big city

❑ a place of interest . . .

whether you want to share materials, give a presentation, or volunteer to read books aloud in class. If you'd like to give a class presentation, plan to bring along photographs, souvenirs, maps, or anything that will give us a clearer picture of a particular place. Please indicate what you'd like to do on the tear-off below, and return. We'd love to share our "Cross Country Trip with Books".

Thank You,
Your Child's Teacher

_____

I _____

_____

_____

_____
(Parent's signature)

Name_____

A Book-Mobile

Take a cross-country trip.
See the sights. Get ready for this adventure.
Design your very own Bookmobile. Be sure to write
your name on your Bookmobile.

My Book Tour

Take a trip... with books.
Keep track of the places
you see.
Make some notes.

Teacher's Note: Cut out these customized BOOKMOBILES to add a creative touch to this reading project and to launch this cross-country tour. Decorate bulletin boards or use with maps of the U.S.A. Publish students' writings on the bookmobile and post on the appropriate map location.

New England

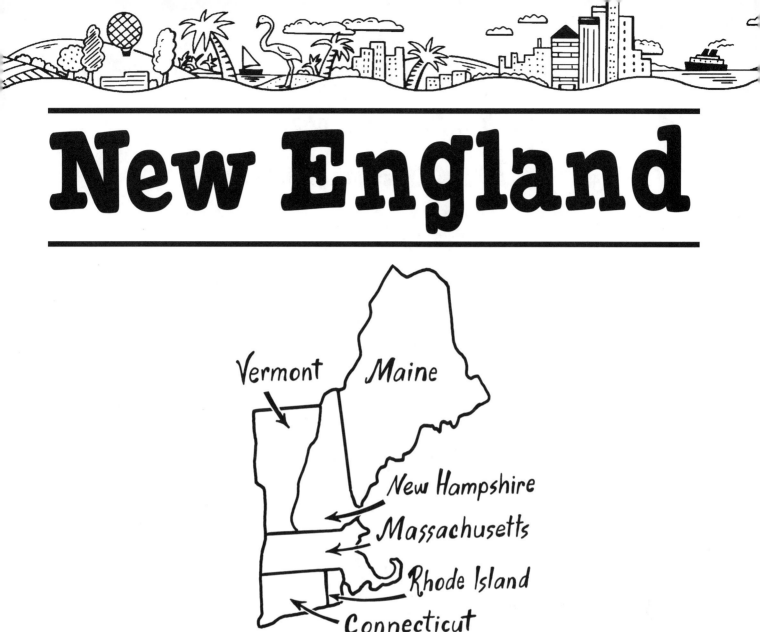

DID YOU KNOW?

▶ that you can learn about our country's very early history in this part of the country...

▶ that there are many lighthouses along the rugged coast of Maine...

▶ that on Cadillac Mountain, in Maine's Acadia National Park, what sounds like thunder is actually the waves hitting the rocks below...

▶ that the poet Robert Frost wrote many poems about the beautiful landscapes of New England...

▶ that people love to visit this area in the fall, because the colorful leaves make such a spectacular sight...

▶ that maple syrup comes from the sugar maple trees...

▶ that Rhode Island is our smallest state...

▶ that you might get to see a moose in the northern part of this region...

Make Way for Ducklings

Robert McCloskey
Viking, 1969

This 1941 Caldecott winner begins, "Mr. and Mrs. Mallard were looking for a place to live." Although Mr. Mallard spotted several possibilities, Mrs. Mallard did not agree. She was not going to raise her children in a neighborhood with foxes in the woods... or turtles in the water. When the ducks finally land, they take readers on a delightful tour of Boston. As the Mallard family searches for the perfect home, this children's classic offers an interesting view of the Boston Public Garden, Beacon Hill, the State House, Louisburg Square, and the Charles River.

Behind The Scenes

While working in the Beacon Hill section of Boston, Robert McCloskey noticed the ducks in the Boston Public Garden. That's how the idea for *Make Way for Ducklings* originated. Once he decided to develop the story, the author learned all he could about mallards. He even bought ducks at a market, so he could observe them and follow them around. Imagine having four ducks living in your bathtub!

Many Different Directions

⭐ **On a map, locate Boston.**
Identify the state and the region of the country that it's in. Point out that this is the state capital. Recall how the ducks in this story, saw Boston. If possible, invite someone who has visited this historic city to come to class and share photographs, souvenirs, and highlights of that trip.

⭐ **Compile a list of "sights to see" in Boston.**
Include places mentioned in the story... and the Freedom Trail, Boston Harbor, the reenactment of the Boston Tea Party, the warship USS Constitution, the birthplace of Ben Franklin, the Children's Museum, etc. Display books and travel brochures, so that students can look for places of interest.. and add to the list.

⭐ **Imitate a writer.** Before writing this book, McCloskey studied, observed, and learned about ducks. As a group, study, observe, and learn about ducks. Use story details and pictures to discover interesting facts about ducks and ducklings. Find out what they eat, where they live, how they move, etc. If possible, take a walk to a local pond to observe the ducks. As a group project, create your own book about ducks and ducklings.

⭐ **Recall the Swan Boat ride described in the story.** Point out that visitors can still go to the Boston Public Garden and enjoy a ride on this boat. Mention that this ride costs money. (For kids under twelve, it's ninety-five cents.) Encourage students to tell about their own experiences at parks. As a group, list "things to do in a park" that cost money. Then, think of activities that are free.

⭐ **Talk about Mr. and Mrs. Mallard looking for a place to live.** Stress the fact that the couple didn't share the same opinions. Write stories about choosing a good place to live—from a duck's point of view... from a pet's point of view... or, from a particular animal's point of view. As children share their stories, help them understand the difference between *needs...* and *wants.*

⭐ **Read more award-winning books by Robert McCloskey.** The Caldecott Honor Book(1952), *One Morning in Maine* and the Caldecott winner(1957), *A Time of Wonder* are both great introductions to the New England area.

11

Name_____

A Place to Live

Mrs. Mallard had to find a good neighborhood for her children.
What was important to her? Name three things.

_____

_____

_____

Pretend you are looking for a new place to live.
What would you like in your neighborhood?
Think about what would be important to you.
Draw it here. You might include a playground, a library, a zoo etc.

Tell what was most important to you. Explain why.

_____

_____

Name_____

Plan a Trip

Boston is a great place to learn about our country's history. Plan a trip to Boston.

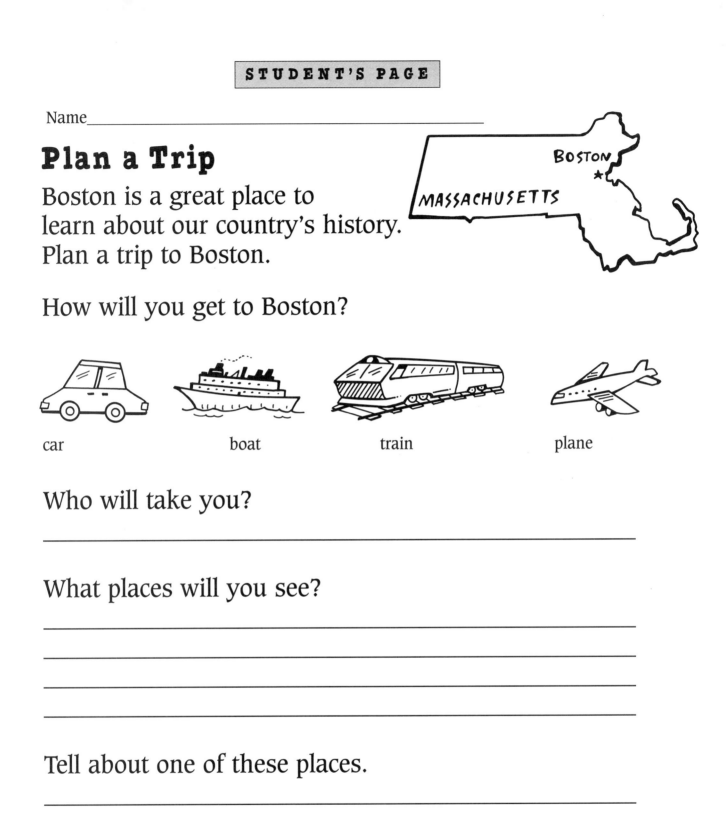

How will you get to Boston?

car   boat   train   plane

Who will take you?

_____

What places will you see?

_____

_____

_____

_____

Tell about one of these places.

_____

_____

Teacher's Note: To plan their trips, students can browse through travel brochures and books about Boston and/or recall places from this story.

Miss Rumphius

Barbara Cooney
Viking, 1982

As a young girl, Alice longs to visit faraway places, and live by the sea. Her grandfather encourages her to also plan to make the world a more beautiful place. When great-aunt Alice grows up to become Miss Rumphius, she travels to exotic locations, settles by the sea, and finds a unique way to add to the beauty of Maine.

Behind The Scenes

Near her home in Maine, Barbara Cooney heard stories about an elderly woman who supposedly lived in the area and threw lupine seeds wherever she went. This "Lupine Lady" was given credit for the fields of lupines scattered all around that part of the country. When the author decided to write a story about that character, she put together pieces of her own life, and that of her family's. Along with her own memories and experiences, she included her travels to exotic places.

Many Different Directions

⭐ **Locate Maine on a map.** Call attention to the coastline, and the many bays, coves, inlets, and tiny islands. Think of sea-related industries, like fishing and lobstering, and how they would be important to people living in this area. Identify the Atlantic Ocean and the other New England states that are along this coast. Learn more about this state. Display books, pictures, travel brochures, and news clippings, about Maine.

by the lake

by the bay

by the river

⭐ **Write "By the Sea" poems.** Imagine what it's like to live by the sea. Describe the sights, the sounds, the smells, and the feelings. Use story details to talk about different settings by the sea. Recall young Alice, living in the city, by the sea... Miss Rumphius, the traveler, visiting a tropical island/fishing village... and Miss Rumphius, settling on the rocky coast. As a group, compile a list of sea-related words. Use these words for the poetry writing activity.

⭐ **Plan a trip to a local florist.** Learn about flowers that are available in your part of the country. On the walk there and back, look for flowers in gardens... in pots... in fields, etc. On a bulletin board, post the names of places where flowers can be found. See how many you can add.

⭐ **Show the power of a flower.** Make your classroom more beautiful. Fill it with all kinds of flowers. Provide a variety of colored paper, tissue paper, fabric scraps, pipe cleaners, markers, and crayons. A paper cup (3 ounce size) can be turned upside down, and used as the flower stand. Suggest that students use their imaginations and see what they create.

⭐ **Read aloud two other books by Barbara Cooney.** *Hattie and the Wild Waves* (another story about a girl who follows her dreams) and *Island Boy* (the author's tribute to Maine). Use these stories to learn more about Barbara Cooney... and Maine.

Name_____

Miss Rumphius

Miss Rumphius loved to travel. Remember the places she visited.

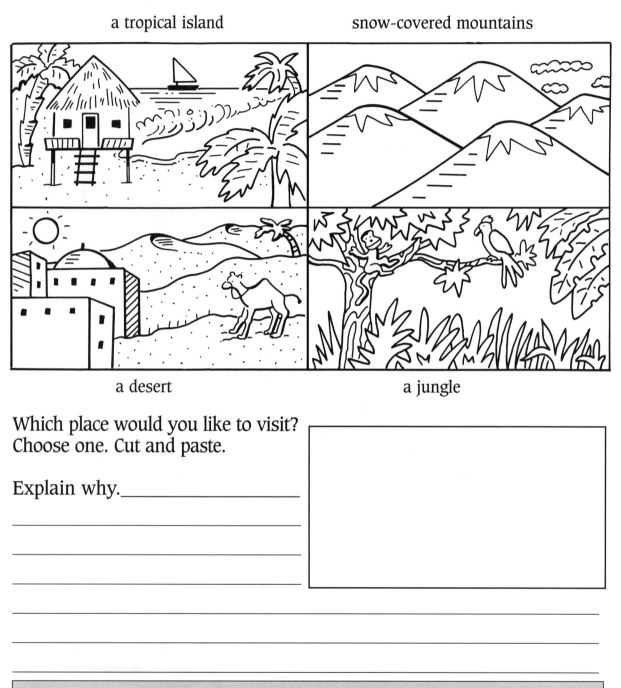

a tropical island   snow-covered mountains

a desert   a jungle

Which place would you like to visit?
Choose one. Cut and paste.

Explain why._____

_____

_____

_____

_____

_____

_____

Teacher's Note: Use this activity to show that different places appeal to different people.

Name_____

Miss Rumphius

Miss Rumphius made
the world more beautiful.
What did she do?

_____

_____

You can make the world more beautiful.
What might you do? List your ideas.

_____

_____

_____

_____

_____

❏ Read the newspaper. ❏ Watch the news. ❏ Talk to your family.
Learn about someone else who made the world more beautiful.
Tell what that person did.

_____

_____

_____

_____

_____

Teacher's Note: Use this activity to demonstrate that one person can make a difference.
Plan time for students to share ideas, news, and interesting stories.

Owl Moon

by Jane Yolen
Scholastic, 1987

On a cold winter's night, beneath a full moon, a young girl and her father trek into the woods to go owling. In a place filled with moonlight, mystery, and magic, father and daughter hope to catch a glimpse of a great horned owl. The poetic style of this 1988 Caldecott winner, along with the exceptional descriptions and illustrations, create a memorable evening in New England.

Behind The Scenes

Jane Yolen, who lives in Massachusetts, dedicates this book to her husband—who took all of her children owling. The story is filled with the sights, the sounds, and the feel of being outdoors on a cold winter's night in the northeast. It captures the excitement of going owling, and the thrill of actually seeing the owl.

Animal watching is a wonderful activity for adults and children to share. In each region of the country, there are exciting possibilites. In this area, whale watching and seal watching are also popular. In fact, Massachusetts is the home of the New Bedford Whaling Museum and the whaling cruise boats that leave from Gloucester or Provincetown.

Many Different Directions

⭐ **On a map, locate Massachusetts.** Point out places of historical significance— Plymouth, Old Sturbridge Village, Concord, Lexington, and Boston. Call attention to Martha's Vineyard, Nantucket, Provincetown, and the Berkshires. Display maps, books, pictures, news clippings, etc. As a group, think of creative ways to gather and share information about this state.

⭐ **Getting the Picture.** Since this story is filled with such wonderful descriptions, use some memorable lines and phrases to create your own pictures. Enable students to make their own discoveries about how words can set the scene. On strips of paper, copy lines, phrases, or sentences from the story. Suggest that children select one strip... read the words, and create their own visual images. You might provide paper, crayons, markers, scraps of material or felt, etc., for the project.

⭐ **Write a "How-to."** As a group, recall important story details that explain how to go owling. Tell how to dress, how to behave, the sounds to make, etc. Help children decide what's important and how to place these tips in the proper sequence.

⭐ **Describe the Great Horned Owl.** Use story details and information to compile a list of what you now know about this creature. Then, create a list of things you'd like to find out about this nocturnal animal. Students can work in pairs or small groups, to gather these facts. Then, they can share these findings with classmates.

Great Horned Owl

We know	We want to know

⭐ **Learn about whale watching.** Since this is also something people do in the Massachusetts area, consider having someone come to class to share their own whale watching experiences. Ask students to imagine how they would feel as they waited to spot a whale. Talk about the thrill of actually seeing a whale swimming in the ocean. Then, find out whether owling or whale watching would be more popular in your class. Ask, if they had their choice, how many children would rather go owling, and how many would rather try whale watching. Post the results.

whale watching	
owl watching	

Name_____

Owl Moon

Go outdoors. Try bird watching.
Be very quiet. Watch the birds.
Draw or Write:

What I saw—

What I heard—

What I felt—

What I thought—

Make a sketch
of a bird you saw.

Name_____

Owl Moon

Share a night time activity with someone in your family.
Wish for something special.

Star light, Star bright
First star I see tonight,
I wish I may,
I wish I might,
have the wish I wish tonight.

Tell about the night.

_____

_____

Tell how the sky looks.

_____

_____

Tell about your wish.

_____

_____

Teacher's Note: Use this home/school activity so students can share the theme of this story with siblings, parents, or grandparents.

Three Days on a River in a Red Canoe

Vera B. Williams
Mulberry, 1981

The "for sale" sign on the red canoe was irresistible. Two cousins and their Moms pooled their money and started planning a three day trip. With its unique format, and wealth of information, this story is packed with maps, routes, camping tips, and sights, that will appeal to kids of all ages. It's a book to be read, again and again.

Behind The Scenes

In her book dedication, this author writes— "Thanks for rivers and friends, big and small." From cooking on a campfire... to putting up a tent... to paddling up the river... to spotting a moose— Vera Williams' unique format captures the scenery, wildlife, and the wonder of the great outdoors.

While attending cooking school in Canada, Williams took up canoeing. During that time, she made many trips with family and friends. A five hundred mile canoe trip along the Yukon River was the inspiration for this story. I showed this book to a noted fishing expert, and after looking over the fish and wildlife, he placed this story in the northeast.

Many Different Directions

Reading a map. As a group, study the map at the beginning of the story. Talk about the the roadways, rivers, symbols, labels, and the trip notes. Ask children to tell about their own experiences with maps. Then, develop a key for this story map. Determine that a wiggly line shows a river. Draw the symbols for a highway, a railroad, a hospital, etc.

river

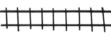

railroad

highway

hospital

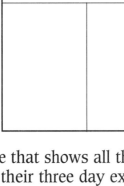

Learn about rivers, big and small. On a map of the U.S., locate and trace the Hudson River, the Delaware River, the Mississippi River, the Grand Canyon River, the Missouri River, etc. Find local rivers, and rivers in different parts of the country. Post your findings on a chart.

RIVERS	
big	small

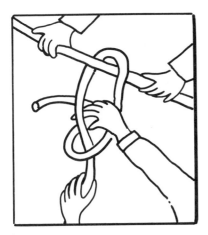

Compile a checklist for this camping trip. Examine the picture that shows all the things these travelers will need for their three day excursion. See how many items children can identify.

Demonstrate how to tie a knot. Bring in a small branch and a piece of rope. Have one child hold the branch, another the rope. Step by step, read aloud the book directions for tying *two half hitches.* Ask the two volunteers to listen carefully, and show each step for the group.

Create your own version of "Go Fish." Cut thirty-two simple fish shapes out of plain oaktag. On each fish, write the name of a fish shown in the story. Make four fish cards for each fish label. Place all the fish in an empty box. Each child can catch a fish... and then, try to learn something about it. Have students decide whether to share these findings— in a bulletin board display... in a group project, book about fish... or as fishing tales.

spotted sunfish

bullhead catfish

redfin pickerel

yellow perch

scale carp

brook trout

black crappie

common white sucker

Name_____

Three Days on a River in a Red Canoe

On camping trips, people cook outdoors.
They plan ahead.
They make simple foods.

Think of something you could cook outdoors.
Keep it simple. Write the recipe.

RECIPE

FOR: _____

FROM THE CAMPSITE OF:_____

YOU'LL NEED:

_____

_____

_____

_____

DIRECTIONS:

_____

_____

_____

_____

Teacher's Note: Cooking outdoors calls for creative thinking. Encourage students to consider the possibilties.

Name_____

Three Days on a River in a Red Canoe

Share something you learned about...

camping

canoeing

fishing

Make your own guide book. Use words and pictures.

by

GUIDE

A

Teacher's Note: From packing... to paddling... to exploring... to pitching a tent, there are many interesting possibilities for these guidebooks.

Middle Atlantic

New York

Pennsylvania

New Jersey

Delaware

Maryland

DID YOU KNOW?

▶ that the Statue of Liberty, which stands in New York Harbor, has been welcoming people into this country for more than a hundred years...

▶ that New York York City is the largest, most famous city in this country...

▶ that at Niagara Falls, in upstate New York, you can take a boat ride underneath the falls...

▶ that New Jersey is called the Garden State, because its land is perfect for agriculture...

▶ that in Philadephia, Pennsylvania, you can see the Liberty Bell, and learn about the Declaration of Independence, and the Constitution...

▶ that everyone should know where the Potomac River and the Chesapeake Bay are...

▶ that a trip to Hershey, Pennsylvania would be a treat for anyone who likes chocolate...

If You Want to Find Golden

Eileen Spinelli
Albert Whitman, 1993

This book takes readers on a colorful tour of a city. By pointing out things that are white... gray... green, this story captures the sights, the sounds, the smells, and the many flavors of a big city. The poetic style and the artwork make exploring new avenues an exciting adventure.

Behind The Scenes

Eileen Spinelli is the wife of Jerry Spinelli, the award-winning children's author. They live in Pennsylvania. In fact, both were born in this state — Eileen, in Philadelphia... Jerry, in Norristown.

In this story, Eileen Spinelli introduces kids to the hustle and bustle of a big city. Her book turns "sight-seeing" into an enjoyable experience for everyone. It's a nice spring board for introducing a colorful city like Philadelphia... and for learning about other interesting cities in the Mid-Atlantic region.

Many Different Directions

⭐ **Make a Story Map.** List all the places students recall from their book tour of this city. Include the street corner, the diner, the greengrocer, etc. As a group, decide how to show these places on a simple street map. Work together to tell this story in a colorful way.

⭐ **Set up a working bulletin board.** Title it: " If You Want To Find Golden." Ask youngsters to fill the board with city sights that are golden. Use magazine or travel brochure pictures, and/or children's drawings. When the board gets full, place all the pictures into a *golden* folder, and start over... with a new color word.

⭐ **Plan a word search**. As you reread this story aloud, encourage youngsters to listen for the compound words. Distinguish between familiar ones, like *rooftops*, *skyscrapers*, and *courthouse*... and unfamiliar ones, such as *morningrise*, and *greengrocer*. Make a list of these words. See how many you can find altogether.

⭐ **Find out how colorful your neighborhood is.** Go on a "If You Want to Find <u>Golden</u>" walk. See how many different things youngsters can discover. By changing the color, and/or the direction of the walk, this activity can be repeated again and again.

⭐ **Learn about some interesting cities.** Start with Philadelphia. Display pictures, brochures, books, and information about this city. Talk about cities that you or your students have visited. Name others that are of interest. Have volunteers interview family members and neighbors who have traveled to(or lived in) big cities. Find out about places of interest, enjoyable activities, and how the city differs from where you live.

⭐ **As a group, set up a model city.** On a small table or desktop, display some buildings, skyscrapers, cars, trucks, etc. To make the buildings, cover mini-juice boxes, tiny raisin boxes, etc., with construction paper. Add matchbox cars, trucks, and other small figures. Encourage students to use their imaginations, and available materials, to plan and create this city scene.

Name_____

If You Want to Find Golden

Make a new game. You will need: crayons, glue, color wheel, oaktag circle, paper clip, paper fastener, scissors.

Color each section. Use different colors. Then, cut out the color wheel. Paste on the oaktag circle. Put a paper fastener in the center with a paper clip for a spine. Spin the paper clip.

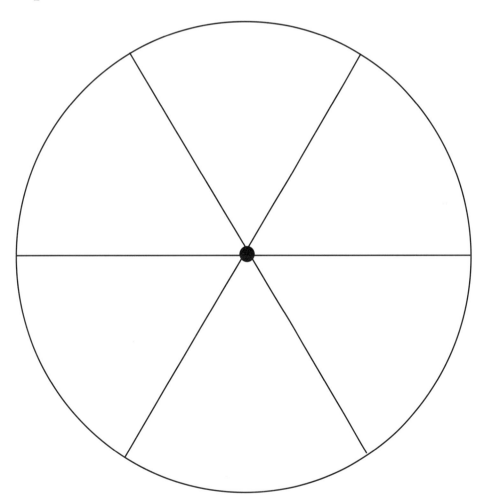

Teacher's Note: Provide pre-cut oaktag circles to back the wheels. Have children use these game wheels along with the student page that follows.

Name_____

Play a Sight-Seeing Game.

Spin the paper clip. Look at the color it stops on.
Think of something you see that's the same color.
Write it in the correct box below.

color	in the city	in the country	in your neighborhood

Teacher's Note: Using the color wheel on the previous page, along with this record-keeping sheet, youngsters create a game that can be played again and again.

Tar Beach

Faith Ringgold
Scholastic, 1991

On a rooftop in Harlem, surrounded by skyscrapers, a young girl named Cassie tells how her family spends hot summer nights in New York. Lying on a mattress, enjoying the sights and sounds while her parents play cards, Cassie shares her views of Tar Beach... the George Washington Bridge... and the city.

Behind The Scenes

Faith Ringgold has lived in Harlem all her life. She is an artist who became interested in storytelling. That's how Ringgold began using quilts as vehicles for her stories. Her *Tar Beach* story quilt was the first of five in her "Woman on the Bridge" series. These quilts are in the collection at the Guggenheim Museum in New York City. Although her *Tar Beach* picture book was inspired by the story quilt, she created new paintings for this story. There is a picture of the original story quilt— courtesy of the Guggenheim— in this book. Use it as a springboard for art appreciation... and an introduction to museums.

Many Different Directions

⭐ **Learn about bridges.** Identify Cassie's bridge. Find out what youngsters learned about the George Washington Bridge from the story. List that information. Point out the difference between fact and opinion. Then, divide youngsters into small groups. Ask each group to gather facts about one of the New York bridges.

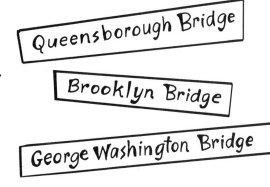

Queensborough Bridge

Brooklyn Bridge

George Washington Bridge

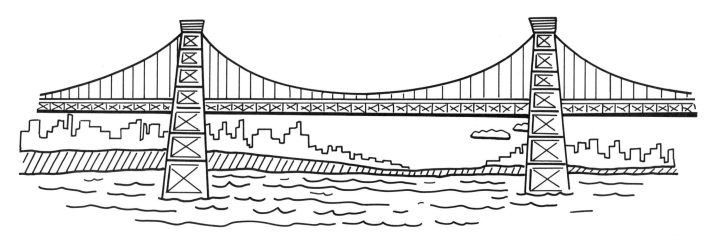

Compile a list of "beach" words. As youngsters brainstorm and free-associate, encourage words other than *tar* and *roof.* However, point out that to many New Yorkers, "tar beach" is a familiar place. (I must admit that I once spent many hot summer days on the roof of my apartment building, sitting in a beach chair sipping a cold lemonade.)

Introduce rooftop gardens. Using the roof scene in the story as a springboard, call attention to the plants along the walls. Mention that many New York apartment dwellers have rooftop gardens. In fact, some are quite elaborate. If possible, show pictures. Develop the idea that in a big city, a rooftop may be the only space available for gardening projects. Imagine living in a big city. Think of other things people might do on their roofs.

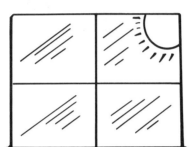

An "On the Roof" bulletin board. From sunbathing... to gardening... to star gazing, show all kinds of activities that families can enjoy on a city rooftop.

Set up a "class" beach. Create your own sandbox. Fill a large container with sand. Display the box in a sunny corner. Place unsharpened pencils, cookie cutters, plastic forks, etc., next to the box. Invite children to play in the sand—making pictures, writing words, or mapping out places of interest.

Read aloud *Abuela,* by Arthur Dorros, another story in which a young girl recalls flying above New York City. The occasional use of Spanish words adds to the sights and sounds of this city adventure.

Name_____

Tar Beach

Picture a sand beach at the ocean. Remember Tar Beach. Tell about them here.

Tar Beach   **A Sand Beach**

Tar Beach		A Sand Beach	
Why Cassie's family goes to this place		Why people go to this place.	
Things the family takes to this place.		Things people take to this place.	

What if you went to Tar Beach? What do you think you would see... hear... smell? Draw it here.

What I would see...	What I would hear...	What I would smell...

What if you went to a sand beach?
What do you think you would see... hear... smell? Draw it here.

What I would see...	What I would hear...	What I would smell...

Name_____

Tar Beach

Let your imagination take you somewhere new.
Make up a place to write about. Choose one.

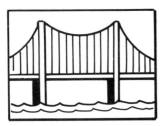
a bridge

a museum

a beach

a skyscraper

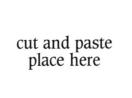

cut and paste
place here

★ Give your place a name. _____

★ Tell where it is located. _____

★ Describe how it looks. _____

_____

★ Tell what makes it special. _____

_____

Teacher's Note: Use this activity as a springboard for artwork and/or creative writing.

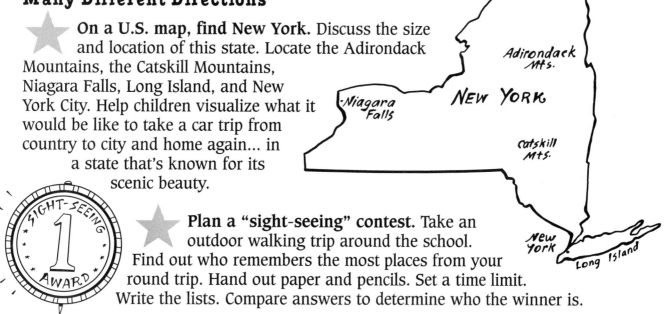

Round Trip

Anne Jonas
Mulberry, 1983

Round *Trip* is a one day trip from country to city and home again.
It's not only a story, it actually is a round trip! Readers go through
the book enjoying the sights, then flip the book over, and see something new on the way back. The black and white drawings and
unique format appeal to kids of all ages. This award-winning book
will definitely change the way children look at things.

Behind The Scenes

Born and raised in New York, Anne Jonas is married to Donald Crews, the well-
known children's author/illustrator. For her, creating unique books is the most
fun. Her sense of adventure is what makes *Round Trip* an interesting story and a
clever visual game.

To create this book, Jonas took pictures of the Manhattan skyline from the
Brooklyn Bridge. She also studied lots of pictures in landscape books.
The possibilities were there. But, to realize them took a lot of trial and error.
Jonas remembers wanting to draw a string of telephone poles that, when turned
upside down, would look like a bridge. She was amazed, when she turned her
drawing over, and it actually worked.

Many Different Directions

On a U.S. map, find New York. Discuss the size
and location of this state. Locate the Adirondack
Mountains, the Catskill Mountains,
Niagara Falls, Long Island, and New
York City. Help children visualize what it
would be like to take a car trip from
country to city and home again... in
a state that's known for its
scenic beauty.

Plan a "sight-seeing" contest. Take an
outdoor walking trip around the school.
Find out who remembers the most places from your
round trip. Hand out paper and pencils. Set a time limit.
Write the lists. Compare answers to determine who the winner is.

Share some interesting views. Recall going to the top of the tallest building and looking down. Mention standing on the street, looking back up at that building. Choose one of these points of view. Imagine what you would see. Write a brief description.

Learn about places of interest. Since 1931, when the project was completed, the Empire State building has been an important landmark. Although it's no longer the city's tallest building, it's still one of the most famous. Share stories about important skyscrapers, landmarks, and well-known buildings in New York City. Places like the World Trade Center, Rockefeller Center, the United Nations, and Wall Street, should appeal to youngsters. Display pictures, facts, and newspaper clippings on an "I Love New York" bulletin board.

Make Black and White Tear Pictures. Have some fun experimenting with paper... and settings. Hand each child one sheet of black paper, one sheet of white, and some paste. By slowly tearing the black paper, youngsters will create hills, mountains, waves, trees, and other interesting possibilities. Pasting these shapes onto the white paper should produce some unique scenes.

Appreciate other artwork. Introduce youngsters to Grandma Moses, who began painting her rural New York scenes at the age of seventy-six or, show realistic street scenes by Edward Hopper, or fantastic views of the city by Georgia O'Keefe— or the British artist Beryl Cook. Examine several pictures and see what kinds of discoveries kids can make. Encourage them to paint or draw their own "New York Scenes."

Name_____

Round Trip

Go on a round trip. Cut and paste the pictures. Tell a story.

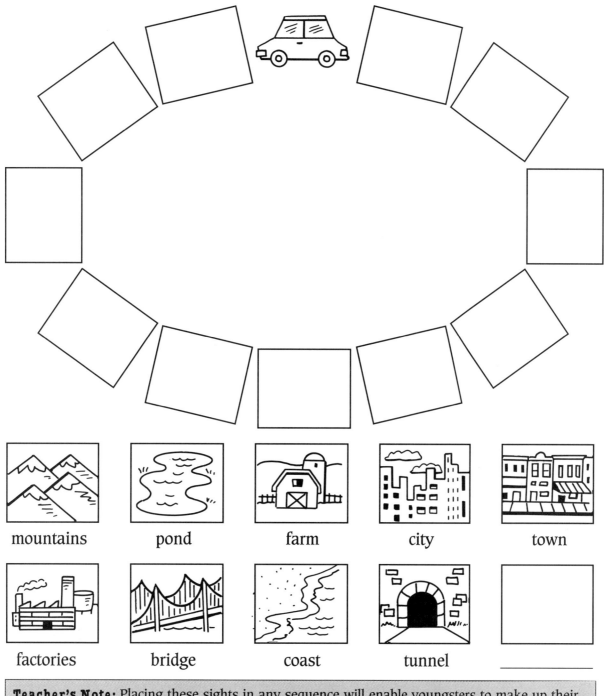

mountains

pond

farm

city

town

factories

bridge

coast

tunnel

_____

Teacher's Note: Placing these sights in any sequence will enable youngsters to make up their own round trip stories. Invite students to fill in last box any way they choose.

Name_____

Round Trip

Cut out the pieces. Place the pictures next to one another. Color the pictures. Make a New York style skyline.

Teacher's Note: By moving these pictures around, and actually seeing the possibilities, youngsters should make their own discoveries about how to create a scene.

Southeast

DID YOU KNOW?

▶ that this part of the country is packed with history...

▶ that there are many beautiful beaches along this coast...

▶ that the Appalachian Mountains, and the Blue Ridge Mountains, are in this region of the country...

▶ that in West Virginia you can take a ride into the side of a mountain on a coal car...

▶ that Nashville, Tennessee is known for its country-and-western music...

▶ that jazz music is played day and night in New Orleans, Louisiana...

▶ that large paddle-wheel boats take people up and down the Mississippi River...

▶ that St. Augustine, Florida, is the oldest city in this country...

▶ that you might see an alligator in the Okefenokee Swamp in Georgia, or in the Florida Everglades...

Bigmama's

Donald Crews
Greenwillow, 1991

Every summer, the author and his family took the train to Cottondale, Florida, to spend time on his grandparents' farm. From going to the train station... to greeting the relatives... to seeing the familiar sights, like the front porch, the well, the toolshed, the barn, and the stable, this autobiographical picture book captures the joy of a favorite place, childhood memories, and country life in this part of the south.

Behind The Scenes

Donald Crews, the award-winning author/illustrator, was born in Newark, New Jersey. Every summer, he and his siblings took the train to Cottondale, Florida—his mother's hometown. Those annual visits, spent on his grandparents' farm, formed some of his fondest childhood memories.

During those summers on his grandparents' farm, Crews became interested in trains. He loved sitting on the front porch, and counting the cars on the trains as they passed by. As a matter of fact, those childhood memories were the inspiration for his book *Freight Trains*.

Many Different Directions

On a map, locate Florida. Identify the bordering states. Determine that Florida is a peninsula, and trace its coastline. Point out the Atlantic Ocean and the Gulf of Mexico. Most likely,(because of its size) Cottondale will not appear on your Florida map. Use the map below to help you pinpoint its location.

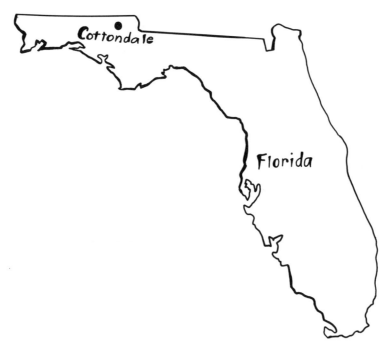

⭐ **Set up a "Sunshine State" exhibit.** Since Florida is known as the "Sunshine State," and one of its major industries is tourism, share information about some of the places that attract visitors. Display books, travel brochures, and information about places such as Epcot, Disney, the Kennedy Space Center, Saint Augustine, etc. Survey the class. Find out how many students have visited any of these places. Encourage those individuals to tell about the trip, and/or bring in photos, souvenirs, etc.

⭐ **Design your own map of Florida.** On large posterboard, sketch the outline of this state. With the group, list the places you want to include on your map. Begin with Cottondale. Add Orlando, Cape Canaveral, Miami, Key Largo, and other places that appeal to children. As a co-operative learning experience, go step by step, through the map-making process. Consult books and maps to determine the exact location of each site. Mark and label the various locations. Use students' creative ideas and suggestions to give the project a personal touch.

⭐ **Take a trip... down memory lane.** Talk about the sewing machine, and the record player that Crews fondly describes. Determine how a sewing machine that you pedal like a bicycle, differs from the kind that children have seen. Compare a wind-up record player to one that you've used in your classroom. Share reactions to the kerosene lamps, the washstand, the well, and anything else that might be unfamiliar to students.

⭐ **Share another author's story about summer visits to the South.** Read aloud *Back Home* by Gloria Jean Pinkney(Dial, 1992), with artwork by her husband, award-winning illustrator Jerry Pinkney. This book is also about a child from up North, who takes the train to Lumberton, North Carolina— her mama's hometown— to spend time on the family farm. Then, compare these two stories... listing the similarities and differences.

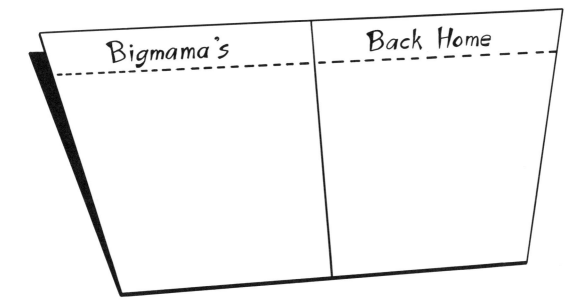

Name_____

Summer Activities

Think about the summer in Cottondale.
Tell about the summer where you live.

What Children Do For Fun

In Cottondale   Where You Live

What Chores Children Can Do

In Cottondale   Where You Live

Teacher's Note: As youngsters compare the two settings, and jot down their ideas, call attention to similarities... and differences.

Name_____

Cottondale Cards

Cut out the "place" cards below. Put them in any order. Make up a story about Cottondale to go with the cards. Tell it to a friend.

the house

the barn

the stable

the pond

the toolshed

COTTONDALE

the train station

Georgia Music

Helen V. Griffith
Greenwillow, 1986

A young girl from Baltimore spends the summer in Georgia with her grandfather. He introduces her to two kinds of music— the kind he plays on his harmonica... and the kind made by the birds, insects, and frogs. After they put on straw hats, work side by side in the garden, and share lazy summer afternoons, the girl gets to know more about her grandfather... nature... and that part of the country.

Behind The Scenes

The idea of a grandfather introducing his grandchild to the wonderful sounds of nature, and to the many songs he plays on his mouth organ, makes this a delightful selection. Use the story as a spring board for a variety of listening activities. Talk about the sounds of birds, insects, the wind, the rain, the ocean, etc. Help children imagine what they'd hear in that Georgia setting... in your area... in a busy city... at the beach... and in other parts of the country.

Many Different Directions

On a map, locate Georgia. Name the states that border it, and trace the coastline. Use the direction words *north, south, east,* and *west* to determine which part of the country it's in. Recall that the girl in the story came to Georgia... from Baltimore. Determine which state Baltimore is in. Then, map out a route from Baltimore to the Georgia border. Show how far one place is, from the other.

⭐ **Find out more about the "Peach State."** Discuss why Georgia is called the "Peach State." Determine how many students have eaten peaches from Georgia. Mention that peanuts are also an important crop from this area. Develop the concept that many things we eat, come from different parts of this country. Compile a list of eight to ten of the most popular fruits and vegetables. Ask pairs of students to work together to find out where each one is grown. Post these findings on a map.

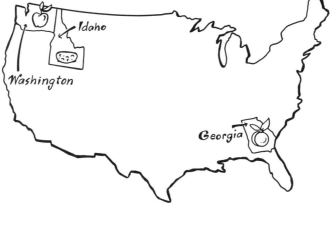

⭐ **Get "a taste of" the south.** Name the things that were grown in grandfather's garden. Since collard greens and black-eyed peas may not be familiar foods, have samples on hand for students to examine. If possible, ask a parent or grandparent to give a cooking demonstration, or prepare a southern dish for youngsters to taste.

⭐ **Listen to another kind of Georgia music.** Play a recording or tape of the popular song, "Georgia on My Mind "(by Ray Charles, Michael Bolton, etc.) Explain that in 1979, the people of Georgia adopted this well-known song, as the official state song. Ask volunteers to gather information about other state songs. Mention that the "Let's Discover the States" series (Chelsea House) or the "America the Beautiful" series (Children's Press) would be useful resources. On a bulletin board, display a large map of the U.S. Invite students to post "musical" notes. Write the names of state songs and place them in the appropriate places.

⭐ **Go on a listening walk.** A quiet stroll outdoors can help children become more "tuned in" to the sounds around them. Encourage youngsters to think about and remember what they hear. Then, return to class, and have everyone jot down what they remember. Allow time for students to share their observations.

Name_____

Georgia Music

There were all kinds of sounds in *Georgia Music*.
Think of some sounds you hear. Can you tell about them?
Make your own sound effects. Use interesting words.

THINK OF...	Write or draw the name.	Write or draw the sound.
a bird		
an insect		
an animal		
a tool		
a musical instrument		

Teacher's Note: As children name something familiar in each category, they can think about the sounds it makes, and write words for those sounds.

Name_____

Georgia Music

The harmonica is a very popular instrument. It fits in a pocket.
It's easy to play. People of all ages can have fun with it.
You can, too. Find out how.

Look at this harmonica.
How many holes does it have? _____ holes.

Some harmonicas have the holes numbered.
This makes it easier to play a tune.
Number the holes on this harmonica.
Go from left to right. Start with the numeral 1.

You can hold a harmonica with one hand or two hands.

   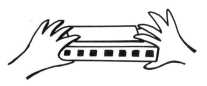

Which one will you try ?   1   2

You can play a harmonica. Try this. Pucker your lips.

Blow into one hole.   Breathe in on the same hole.

What do you think will happen to the sound? _____

_____

Teacher's Note: Make children aware of the fact that this musical instrument is inexpensive...
portable... and can be played without lots of practicing or music lessons.

The Relatives Came

Cynthia Rylant
Scholastic, 1985

Every summer, the relatives came for a visit and filled the house with lots of hugging, laughing, and breathing. This Caldecott Honor book captures the excitement of a family reunion... and the pleasures of going on a vacation. Packing up the car at four in the morning is the perfect beginning to that long scenic drive... from Virginia.

Behind The Scenes

Cynthia Rylant was born in Hopewell, Virginia. She grew up in West Virginia, and shares much of what happened to her there in her books.

The way she captures the simple pleasures in life— like being reunited with relatives— is what makes this book an enjoyable experience for readers of all ages. Plus, the idea of visiting relatives is a great vehicle for traveling to new places and unfamiliar parts of the country.

★ Class Survey ★

Williamsburg	✓	✓	✓	✓			
Jamestown	✓	✓	✓	✓	✓		
Mount Vernon	✓	✓					
Monticello	✓	✓	✓	✓	✓	✓	
Arlington	✓	✓					

Many Different Directions

⭐ **On the map, find Virginia.**
Discuss its size and location. Use story details and picture clues to spark interest in this part of the country. Share a bit of history by pointing out places like Williamsburg, Jamestown, Mount Vernon, Monticello, and Arlington. Display books, maps, pictures, and travel brochures, that provide information about them. Then, take a class survey. Find out how many students would like to visit each place.

⭐ **On a map of Virginia, trace the Blue Ridge Mountains.** Mention that from a distance, the ridges of these mountains appear to be shades of blue. Because the forests along these mountainsides are so dense, they affect the color. Invite some creative thinking. Have youngsters write original stories, explaining how the mountains got their name.

⭐ **Make a "Guest Book."** Compile a list of things the relatives did together. Using the text and picture clues, youngsters can recall how they worked, played, and had a wonderful time. Name different things that people can do when relatives and/or friends visit. Then, create your own "Guest Book." Students can illustrate activities that people of all ages can enjoy— at gatherings... outings... or special occassions.

⭐ **Design a "Welcome" Mat.** People have different ways of welcoming visitors into their homes(or classrooms). Recall what happened in the book when "the relatives came." Think of other ways to make visitors feel welcome. Ask students to make "collage-type" welcome mats. By cutting pictures, letters, and words, out of old magazines, and arranging them on a large sheet of paper, children can extend the theme of this story.

⭐ **Plan a car trip.** Display a simple road map. As a group, choose a destination. Find the simplest way to reach that point. Then, map out the route. Determine whether this trip will be long or short. Name some things you expect to see along the way.

⭐ **Make Travel Folders.** Have kids share their favorite car/traveling games by contributing a page to a class book. Ask each child to write a description or explanation of a game or activity that can be enjoyed while riding in the car. From "I Spy... " to "Alphabet Games, " suggest that children include simple directions and pictures. Make copies of each submission so that kids can place them inside the activity booklets they design.

Name_____

The Relatives Came

Think about visiting someone you know.

Who would you like to visit? _____

Where would you go? _____

How would this place differ from where you live?_____

_____

Who would go with you? _____

How would you get there? _____

What would you do to get ready for the trip? _____

_____

_____

What would you pack?
Draw it here.

Teacher's Note: Whether this questionnaire is filled out by students, or used in an interview, it shows how to plan ahead.

Name_____

She'll Be Comin' Round The Mountain

Try singing these verses.

She'll be comin' round the mountain   ...   when she comes.

She'll be comin' round the mountain   ...   when she comes.

She'll be comin' round the mountain,
She'll be comin' round the mountain,
She'll be comin' round the mountain, ...   when she comes.

Add some of your own ideas.

She'll be riding seven horses   ...   when she comes.
Oh, we'll all go down to meet her   ...   when she comes.
She'll be wearing red pajamas   ...   when she comes.
She'll be _____ when she comes...

Teacher's Note: Have a sing along! Kids can make a music/story connection and add some of their own words or phrases to this well-known American song.

When I Was Young in the Mountains
Cynthia Rylant
Penguin, 1982

As the author reminisces about her childhood days in the mountains, she takes us to the swimming hole... the outdoor well... the country store... the old schoolhouse... and the coal mines, where her grandfather worked. This Caldecott winner captures that sense of family, warmth, and peace, that can be found in the Appalachian Mountains of West Virginia.

Behind The Scenes

Cythnia Rylant grew up in West Virginia. From the age of four, until she was eight, Rylant lived with her grandparents in Cool Ridge. Her grandfather was a coal miner, and actually worked in the mines since he was nine years old. In this story, Rylant shares her memories of life in the moutains and recalls the simplest pleasures... like shelling beans on the front porch.

Both *The Relatives Came* and *When I Was Young in the Mountains* are available on filmstrip(Random House).

Many Different Directions

On a map, find West Virginia. Talk about the size, shape, and location of this state. Mention that West Virginia is known as the Mountain State. Gather pictures that show the mountains, steep hills, and rugged landscape of this area. As a group, collect facts and information for a guided tour of West Virginia.

Make an interactive chart for *"When I was young in the mountains."* Place blank cards nearby. Invite students to think of places they enjoyed when they were younger. Ask them to make word cards for each. See how many different places kids can name.

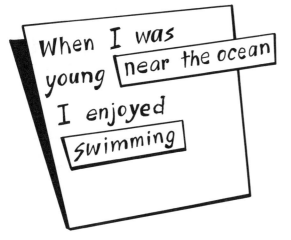

★ **Share "When I Was Young..." stories.** Have youngsters close their eyes and remember a place they loved to go. Ask students to show you that place using words and pictures.

★ **Put up your own Traveling Photographer sign.** Recall the traveling photographer in this story. Talk about the role of the traveling photographer in the early days of this country. Determine how important it was to capture special moments on film. Then, set up your own bulletin board display. Invite youngsters to contribute photos showing a place they traveled to. Have students write brief captions to go with the photos.

★ **Get "a taste" of one of the foods grown in West Virginia.** Since corn is an important crop, talk about the hot cornbread mentioned in the story.

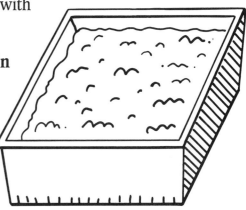

Describe how cornbread looks, smells, tastes. Ask how it is made. Then, make (or bring in) cornbread. Serve it with pinto beans or okra. Not only is this a nice story connection, it gives youngsters the opportunity to try something new.

★ **Set up a country store.** Use the picture in the book as a springboard. Make a list of things you'll need. Brown bags and/or white pillow cases can be used as sacks. Empty boxes and canisters can be labeled. One or two aprons, and a simple scale will enable youngsters to enjoy this play center.

Name_____

A Change of Scenery

Cut out the pictures. Paste them on oaktag cards. Change the scenes. Tell a story.

Teacher's Note: By simply changing the scenes, youngsters have props to help them retell this story... or make up their own.

Name_____

When I Was Young in the Mountains

Make a mini-book. Read the words on these pages.
Add the pictures. Share your book with others.

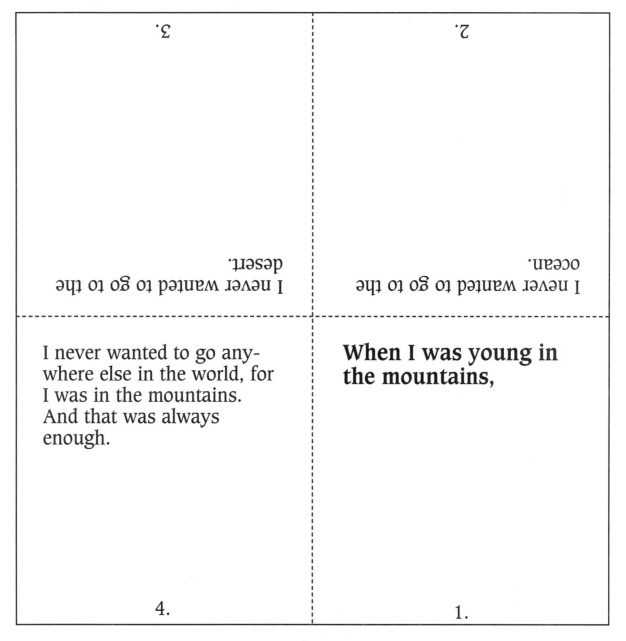

3.

I never wanted to go to the
desert.

2.

I never wanted to go to the
ocean.

I never wanted to go any-
where else in the world, for
I was in the mountains.
And that was always
enough.

**When I was young in
the mountains,**

4.

1.

Teacher's Note: Invite students to cut on the solid lines and fold on the dotted lines, greeting-card style, to make a mini-book. As youngsters make and share these mini-books, they will discover that each person pictures a place in a different way.

Appalachia: The Voices of Sleeping Birds

by Cynthia Rylant
Harcourt Brace, 1991

From the beauty of the mountains to the coal mines below, Cynthia Rylant takes us on a guided tour of *Appalachia*. Using a warm, friendly style, the author shares the sights, sounds, and smells. From day to day life, to the seasonal changes, this book offers a wonderful view of West Virginia.

Behind The Scenes

Cynthia Rylant grew up in West Virginia. Between the ages of four and eight, she lived with her grandparents. Her grandfather had been a coal miner since he was a young boy.

Rylant's picture book *When I Was Young in the Mountains*, offers another look at Appalachia, and can be used as a story connection.

The introduction to this book— which happens to be an excerpt from James Agee's *Knoxville: Summer 1915*— should also be read aloud more than once.It explains the significance of the title and it's a nice way to show how one writer influences another... and how easy it is to move from place to place.

Many Different Directions

On a map, find West Virginia. Talk about the size, the shape, and the location of this state. Mention that West Virginia is known as the Mountain State. Gather pictures that show the mountains, steep hills, and rugged landscape of this place. Explain that Appalachia refers to the area between the Allegheny Highland in the Appalachian Mountains, and the Allegheny Plateau. As a group, collect facts and information about West Virginia... and coal mines.

Locate Knoxville, Tennessee on a map. Determine which region of the country this state is in and, where it is in relation to West Virginia. Barry Moser, the illustrator of this book, was raised in Tennessee. Read aloud "About the Illustrator" on the last page of the book. Display books, pictures, and brochures on Tennessee. Spotlight the Great Smoky Mountains, Chattanooga, Knoxville, and Nashville.

★ *Nashville*

TENNESSEE

★ **Take a class survey.** Mention that some people never leave Appalachia. Explain that those who do often come back. Develop the concept that some people live in the same place for their whole lives. Others may move around often. Survey the class. Find out how many youngsters have lived in the same place since they were born. Determine how many moved once since birth. Ask how many moved more than once. Show your findings on a pictograph.

★ **Plan a book talk.** Read aloud *When I Was Young in the Mountains*, Rylant's Caldecott winner that captures the pleasures of growing up in Appalachia. Consider why this author uses the same setting for different stories. Display *But I'll Be Back Again: An Autobiography* by the Newberry Award winning Author (Cynthia Rylant, Beech Tree, 1993). Mention that in this book, Rylant tells about growing up in rural West Virginia, and explains where some of her book ideas came from.

★ **Share details on Appalachia.** Talk about how authors use words to take readers to places they remember. Then, see what students remember about Appalachia. Have them think of words that can be use under each heading.

Appalachia

the people	the homes	the scenery	the food

Name_____

Appalachia: The Voices of Sleeping Birds

Re-read the introduction to this book.
Think about the title of the story.
Picture Knoxville, Tennessee... in summer. Share a poem.

Knoxville, Tennessee

I always like summer
best
you can eat fresh corn
from daddy's garden
and okra
and greens
and cabbage
and lots of
barbecue
and buttermilk
and homemade ice-cream
at the church picnic

and listen to
gospel music
outside
at the church
homecoming
and go to the mountains with
your grandmother
and go barefooted
and be warm
all the time
not only when you go to bed
and sleep
      — Nikki Giovanni

Teacher's Note: Appreciate the different styles that writers use to tell about a place. Encourage youngsters to share this poem with family members.

Name_____

Appalachia: The Voices of Sleeping Birds

Think about Appalachia in winter... in spring...
in summer... in fall. Draw what you might see below.
Think about where you live. Draw what you see below.

Appalachia   Where You Live

summer	summer
winter	winter
spring	spring
fall	fall

Teacher's Note: To appreciate seasonal changes in different parts of the country, have young-sters make their own observations.

The Story of the White House

Kate Waters
Scholastic, 1991

A visit to the White House, Washington D. C., and our nation's capital— one of the highlights of this cross-country tour. This award-winning book is packed with so much information, it will probably take days to appreciate it all. From the maps, sketches, photographs, and drawings, to all of the fascinating details, this place should capture everyone's attention.

Behind The Scenes

Each year, millions of people go to Washington, D. C. On any given day, as many as ten thousand visitors may tour the White House. The President's home, located at 1600 Pennsylvania Avenue, is just one of many sights to see. Stories about this city, the White House, the government buildings, the Presidents, and important events, should spark interest in history, government, legal issues, and even White House Ghosts.

Many Different Directions

⭐ **Locate Washington, D. C. on a map.** Identify the bordering states and the Potomac River. Talk about the nation's capital and encourage children to share what they know about this place. As a group, examine the map at the beginning of the story. Find the White House, the Library of Congress, the Smithsonian, the Lincoln Memorial, etc.

⭐ **Set up a "Washington News Bureau."** As an ongoing project, post items of interest on a bulletin board. Display newspaper headlines, photos, and articles about the capital, the White House, the President, the First Lady, new laws, important visitors, etc. To give children credit for the material they bring in, have them write their names on an official Press Pass.

★ **Learn about city planning.** Note that Washington is one of the few cities in the world that was actually designed before it was built. Talk about the advantages of planning ahead. Compile a list of decisions that had to be made. If possible, invite a local city planner to visit the classroom to talk about his/her job, and to share information about your city or town.

★ **Plan a contest.** When it was time to decide what kind of house to build for the president, Thomas Jefferson suggested having a contest. This contest was advertised in newspapers all over the country. Imagine what that ad looked like... and what it said. Ask children to submit the ads they picture. Post all the ads, and then choose the winner(s).

★ **Imagine working in Washington.** Think of some of the more exciting possibilities. Use story details to compile a list of job opportunities. Ask each youngster to choose one career(job) and do research on that subject. Encourage them to find out about the education and training needed for each position... along with the responsibilties, salaries, hours, and rewards. Then, schedule a career day. Allow time for youngsters to share their findings.

★ **On the lighter side, read aloud *Arthur Meets the President* by Marc Brown,** another story about a contest and a trip to Washington, D. C.

Name_____

The Story of The White House

Take a trip around Washington, D. C.
Make a sight-seeing wheel.

You'll need scissors and a
paper fastener.
Cut out the two circles.
Cut out the little windows, also.
Place the window circle on top
of the other circle.

Washington Monument

The Capitol

Lincoln Memorial

White House

Put a paper fastener
in the center.
Spin the wheel slowly.
Take a peek at some
places of interest.

Teacher's Note: To make this visual aid, place the wheel with the open windows on top of the
wheel with the pictures and attach them in the center with a paper fastener.

Name_____

The Story of The White House

Some people think the White House is haunted.
They say ghosts of famous people have been
spotted in different rooms.
Plus, there have been reports of mysterious
creaks, groans, and noises. What do you think?
Draw and write about the White House. Tell a ghost story.

3. (upside down)	2. (upside down)
4.	My White House Ghost Story By _____ 1.

Teacher's Note: Invite students to cut on the solid lines and fold on the dotted lines, greeting-card style, to make a mini-book. Display these mini-books in the library corner. Share lots of ghost stories with the same setting.

Midwest

DID YOU KNOW?

► that there are acres and acres of flat prairies and plains in this part of the country...

► that farming is very important here...

► that this region grows more corn and grain than any other place in the world...

► that Chicago is the largest city in the Midwest...

► that the state of Michigan is divided into two parts...

► that four of the five Great Lakes are in this region...

► that at Mount Rushmore, South Dakota, the heads of four American Presidents are carved into a 6,000 foot mountain...

► that Minnesota is known as the Land of 10,000 Lakes...

► that because of the rock formations, it's difficult to travel through North Dakota's Badlands...

In the Tall, Tall Grass

Denise Fleming
Henry Holt and Company, 1991

This award-winning book takes you on a backyard tour from the middle of the day on into early evening. With its simple rhyming text and spectacular artwork, it helps youngsters discover the sights, the sounds, and the many surprises... that can be seen *In the Tall, Tall Grass.*

Behind The Scenes

Denise Fleming and her daughter Indigo, spent many summer afternoons together— in the woods and fields near their home in Ohio. That's how this story idea developed. The hot sun, the sounds of the bees, the birds in the bushes, the ants, the bunnies, the moles, the grasshoppers, the fireflies— everything comes alive on this colorful trip around the yard. This is Fleming's first book where she used pulp painting— a special kind of papermaking. Since this kind of art involves more physical work (transporting buckets of water, beating the pulp, and mixing vats of color) and the creative part has an element of surprise to it (the artist doesn't have complete control over the results), use the book to take a closer look at the beauty of natural settings... and to learn about new ways to use natural resources.

Many Different Directions

On a map, locate Ohio. Name the bordering states. Point out some of the major cities, such as Cleveland, Columbus, Toledo, Dayton, and Cincinnati. Learn about nature and the environment. Post information about the state bird(the Cardinal)... insect(the Ladybug)... tree (Buckeye)... and flower(carnation). Gather pictures of other kinds of birds, animals, flowers, and trees that might be seen around the state.

⭐ **Take a nature walk.** With the group, stroll around your area. Notice the sights, the sounds, and the colors. Suggest that each youngster choose one tree, bird, insect, flower, or animal and study it carefully. Ask children to make a list of words that describe the chosen object. See how many words children can think of.

⭐ **Experiment with paper.** Give each child a piece of green construction paper, scissors, and pipe cleaners. Show them how to cut into the paper again and again... to make tall, tall grass. Then, students can use the grass as a story prop. Using the pipe cleaners, they can make and hide an ant, a snake, a beetle, etc. in the grass.

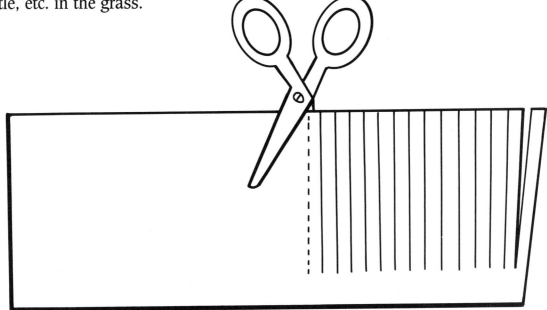

⭐ **Fill a bulletin board with "tall tall grass."** Recreate the story setting. With the group, make a list of all the birds, animals, and insects seen in the grass. Have youngsters volunteer to make caterpillars, snakes, beetles, bees, etc. and put them on display.

⭐ **Make a Nature Booklet.** Youngsters can choose one of the creatures they saw in *In the Tall Tall Grass* and learn more about it. See what children can find out about snakes, fireflies, beetles, etc. Have them write short reports. Assemble these in a class booklet.

⭐ **Read aloud two other books by Denise Fleming.** *In the Small, Small Pond*, offers a look at wildlife and the change of seasons. *Barnyard Banter* makes a trip around the farm a memorable one.

Name_____

In the Tall, Tall Grass

Think about the story. Remember what you saw.
Look around your yard or neighborhood.
Tell what you see. Use words or pictures.

	In the story	Near my home
insects		
birds		
animals		

Remember sounds you liked in the story. Write some of those words.

_____

Listen to the sounds you hear outdoors. Write words for those sounds.

_____

Teacher's Note: This looking/listening activity extends the theme of the story and encourages youngsters to appreciate the sights and sounds.

Name_____

Choose your own ending.

Think of another place. Write the word.

In the tall, tall _____

Pretend you are looking around this place.
Imagine what you would see.

_____

_____

Show how the place looks. Draw it here.

Teacher's Note: By replacing the word "grass," children can let their imaginations take them to many different places.

Mole's Hill: A Woodland Tale

Lois Ehlert
Harcourt Brace, 1994

Mole lives near a pond in the woodlands of Wisconsin. Her safe, comfortable, underground burrow is her favorite place— home. Unfortunately, the local animals are planning a new path to the pond, and Mole's hill is in the way. When Mole learns that she'll have to move, a clever idea enables her to save her home.

Behind The Scenes

This story, set in the woodlands of Wisconsin, was inspired by "When Friends Fall Out"— an American Indian tale that the author remembered hearing. All of the animals, plants, flowers, and trees pictured in this story are indigenous to the area. Interestingly, the illustrations are based upon two popular art forms of the Woodland Indians. The patterns and motifs from hand-sewn beadwork and ribbon applique add to the beauty of this story.

Many Different Directions

Wisconsin

Locate Wisconsin on a map. Discuss the size, shape, and location of this state. As a group, gather interesting facts, pictures, news articles, books, travel folders, about this place. Find out why the state is nicknamed the "Badger State." Discover why it's also called "America's Dairyland." Set up a display.

Explore the woodlands of Wisconsin. Note that the northern part of the state is covered with forests. Point out that both evergreens and leafy trees grow there. Imagine how this area looks in fall, when the leaves change. Recall which woodland animals were in this story. Find out which other animals live in this part of the country. Make a chart.

Woodland Animals:		
Mole	Fox	Skunk

★ **Make "PLACE CARDS."** On 3" x 5" oaktag cards, write one key word from the story— *hill, tunnel, path*, and *pond.* Illustrate the word on the back of each card. As an ongoing project, youngsters should enjoy creating their own sets of place cards, to use for flashcards, matching activities and games.

★ **Read aloud the book *Moon Rope*, another Lois Ehlert tale about a mole, a fox, and a distant place.** Ehlert's version of this Peruvian folktale is written in both English and Spanish. It offers a delightful explanation of why moles dig tunnels and hide. Plus, in this book, the illustrations were inspired by Peruvian artwork. Help youngsters compare the two stories, as you focus on similarities... and differences.

★ **Compile a list of things you learned about moles.** Use story details to determine where they live, what they do, what they eat, etc.

★ **Create an OVER THE HILL bulletin board.** Introduce the art of collage. Point out that Lois Ehlert often uses this technique to illustrate her stories. Take time to appreciate the pictures of *Mole's Hill*. Examine the colorful circles, rectangles, hearts, etc, used to create the different flowers, trees, and plants. Then, watch your own hill take shape. Using construction paper, scissors, and glue, students can make a variety of flowers, trees, and plants, and display them all "over the hill."

Name_____

Mole's Hill

Dear Mole,
Meet us tonight
at the maple tree.

Fox ˙Skunk Raccoon

Fox, Skunk, and Raccoon sent this note. Show where they will meet.

Write a note to a friend. Choose a good place to meet. Tell where and when.

Dear _____,

_____

_____

_____

Teacher's Note: Plan time for children to share these notes. Encourage them to discover some new places right in their own neighborhoods.

Name_____

Mole's Hill

Follow the directions. Make a place to remember.

❑ Put some fish in the pond.

❑ Cover the hill with grass.

❑ Draw flowers and plants on the hill.

❑ Put Fox next to the big tree.

❑ Draw Skunk on the path.

Teacher's Note: In this activity, students follow step-by-step directions and add their own creative touches to a story setting.

Thunder Cake

Patricia Polacco
Scholastic, 1990

On a hot, summer day, on a farm in Michigan, a young girl overcomes her fear of thunderstorms. Her Grandma shows her how. Making "Thunder Cake" is the secret. All the ingredients must be gathered, mixed, and in the oven... before the storm arrives. That's the only way to make an authentic cake. As the two rush around gathering ingredients, readers get a taste of life on a farm... and a peek at the weather.

Behind The Scenes

Patricia Polacco was born in Lansing, Michigan. As a young child, she spent the school year living on a small farm in Union City, Michigan, with her mother and grandparents, and the summers with her father in Williamston, Michigan. Sharing childhood memories is something this author loves to do. The farm in Michigan, stormy weather, grandma, and baking a cake— with just the right ingredients, Polacco shows the magic in an ordinary day. Gathering fresh eggs, milk, tomatoes, and strawberries adds a nice "flavor" to this story.

Many Different Directions

Locate Michigan on a map. Note that this state is divided into two parts. Identify the surrounding states and the Great Lakes. Display books, travel folders, and facts about this state. Talk about the farm in this story. Then, learn about farming in Michigan. As a group project, make an agricultural map. Find out about important crops. Design symbols for each. Tell a farm story. Present this information on a state map.

★ **Show children how to read weather maps.** Bring in a map from a local newspaper. Study the map, the legend, and the different kinds of information given on the page. Help youngsters realize that they can find out about the weather in your area... around the country... and in other parts of the world. To encourage students to check the newspaper regularly, give daily assignments. Have them find the high or low temperature... the rainfall... the storm activity— for a specific place.

★ **Compile a list of hiding places.** Talk about being afraid... of lightning, thunder, storms. Recall that the girl in the story hid under the bed when she was frightened. Think of other places children might hide. Then, name activities that could help you forget about being afraid— making thunder cake, whistling, etc. This list could be used as a springboard for creative writing.

> **Hiding Places:**
> • **under the bed**
> • **under the covers**
> • **in the closet...**

★ **Write a "How To."** Record Grandma's special formula for calculating how far away the storm was. List the directions, step by step.

Begin counting when you see lightning. Count slowly.
Stop counting when you hear thunder.
That number tells how many miles away the storm is.

★ **Learn more about weather and folklore.** Interview parents and relatives. Find out about interesting signs, predictions, and beliefs. As children share this information, talk about reliability, accuracy... and how people are affected by storms.

Name_____

A Weather Watch

Sometimes, you can predict what will happen.
Sometimes, you can't. Keep track of the weather where you live.
Describe what you see in the morning, in the
afternoon, and at night. Make your own Weather Chart.

A Weather Chart

	morning	afternoon	night
Monday			
Tuesday			
Wednesday			
Thursday			
Friday			
Saturday			
Sunday			

Teacher's Note: Plan time for youngsters to share observations and to compare some of the descriptive words they used.

Name_____

Thunder Cake

Some people go to the store to buy food.
Others have everything they need on their farm.
Name some ingredients that the girl and her grandma gathered.
Make a list.

From the farm...

❑ _____   ❑ _____

❑ _____   ❑ _____

❑ _____   ❑ _____

What would you make with these ingredients?
Give this dish a name. Write the recipe.

_____

Ingredients

_____ _____ _____
_____ _____ _____

Recipe

_____
_____
_____

Teacher's Note: In this activity, youngsters will think of creative ways to use available resources.

In Coal Country

by Judith Hendershot
Alfred A Knopf, 1987 (Scholastic)

What's it like growing up in a small Ohio coal mining town? This award-winning book provides an interesting picture of a different way of life. Told with simple text, and wonderful illustrations, a young girl shares her memories of day to day life, seasonal changes, family, and having fun. Her story clearly shows how living near the mines affects the people... and the environment.

Behind The Scenes

Judith Hendershot grew up in Neffs, Ohio— a place near Willow Grove, the setting for this story. Both her father and her grandfather worked in the coal mines. Her memories of growing up in a coal mining town, along with some of her parents' childhood memories, enabled her to write this story. This book— Hendershot's first— has received many awards.

Cynthia Rylant's *When I Was Young in the Mountains* is another book about growing up in a small coal mining town. The story, set in West Virginia, can be used as a literature connection.

Many Different Directions

⭐ **Locate Ohio on a map.** Trace the Ohio River. Note why this river was mentioned in the story. Display books and information on Ohio and its natural resources— coal, clay, limestone, natural gas, petroleum, etc. Have students share what they learned about mining, transporting, and using coal. Jot down these facts. Then, think of other things they'd like to know.

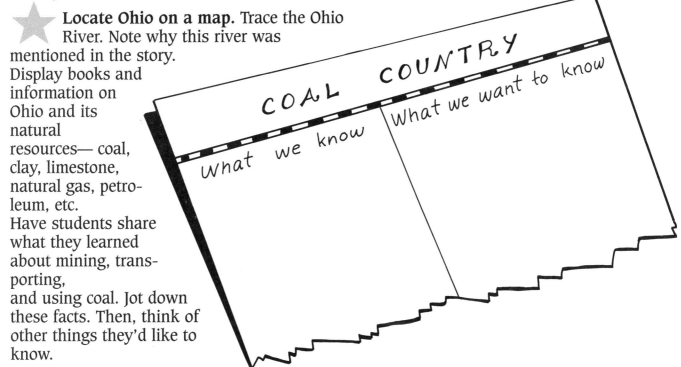

COAL COUNTRY

What we know | What we want to know

⭐ **Call attention to environmental issues.** Recall story details showing the effects of local mining. Create a realistic picture of what it was like living in a coal mining town. List some of the visible signs.

- houses don't look clean
- paint peeling off the houses
- unpleasant smell in the air
- creek water is black (not clear)

⭐ **Create an interactive chart.** Use the title/phrase "in <u>coal</u> country" on a pocket chart. Make the word *coal* replaceable. Place blank cards next to the chart. See how many other words youngsters can think of.

⭐ **Take a closer look at some of the places mentioned in this story.** On a bulletin board, post road signs that point to the creek... the hollow... the grove... the ridge... the spring... the falls... the mine. Ask youngsters to show you around Willow Grove. Have them draw pictures of these places and add them to the display.

⭐ **Read *When I Was Young in the Mountains*** by Cynthia Rylant aloud. Reread *In Coal Country*. Compare and contrast the two books. Decide how they are alike... how they are different.

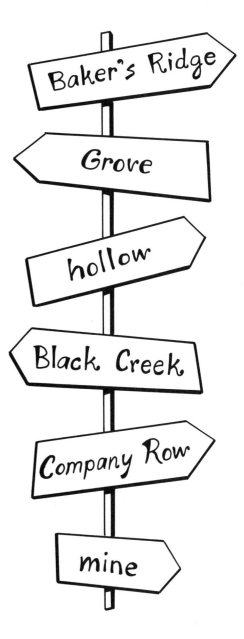

Name_____

In Coal Country

People work in all kinds of places. Think about a coal miner's job.
Think about a job you would like to do, when you grow up.

Write the name of that job in the space below.
Then, tell what you know about each job.

A Coal Miner

where you work		
what you wear		
the hours you work		
the things you like most about the job		
the things you like least about the job		

Teacher's Note: Talk about other jobs mentioned in this story— brakeman, paddy man, engineer, mother. Learn about the different places where people work.

Name_____

In Coal Country

Think about what the children in the story did for fun.
What games did they play? Where did they play them?

king of the mountain   hopscotch   mumbletypeg

Which game would you like to play?

_____

Where could you play this game?

_____

Who would you play with?

_____

How would you play? Explain the rules you would follow.

_____
_____
_____
_____
_____

Teacher's Note: This activity will enable students to share ideas about interesting places...
to play games.

Southwest

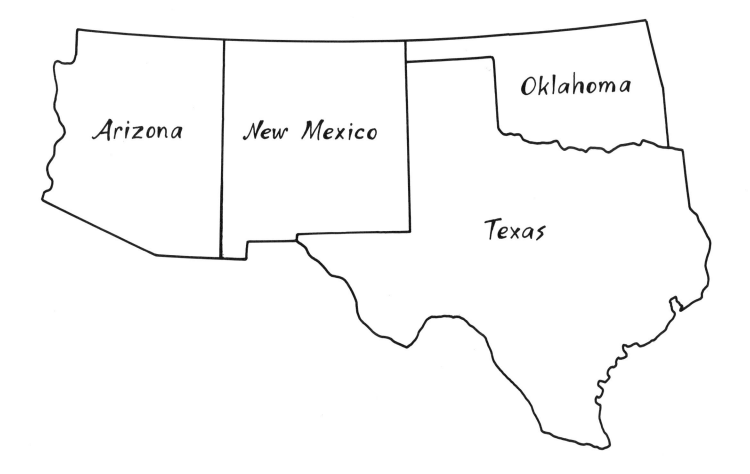

Arizona

New Mexico

Oklahoma

Texas

DID YOU KNOW?

▶ That Texas is the largest state in the contiguous United States (Alaska is the largest, overall)
▶ That the deepest well in the United States is a gas well in Washita County, Oklahoma...
▶ That Arizona's name is thought to be from an Aztec word, *Arizuma*, which means, "silver-bearing"...
▶ That you can visit the ruins of the ancient Pueblo of Pecos, in New Mexico...

Roxaboxen

Alice McLerran
Scholastic, 1991

On a rocky hill, at the corner of Eighth Street and Second Avenue, in Yuma, Arizona, there's a place called Roxaboxen. Created by children, this magical world began with one street... and, over time, grew into a charming little town. The houses, main street, the town hall, the bakery, and the two ice cream parlors were set up years ago, in the middle of a desert setting. Using stones, wooden boxes, colored glass, and lots of imagination, a group of kids built a place to treasure.

Behind The Scenes

This is a true story. In fact, the author's mother was one of the children who actually created the "town" of Roxaboxen. McLerran used an old manuscript written by her mother, along with old letters, maps, and memories from former residents of the area... as background material for this book. McLerran recreated her mother's favorite place... and the magic of children.

Barbara Cooney made two trips to the desert before beginning the illustrations for this book. She considered this to be one of her most difficult assignments. Luckily, the artist found a model hill with rocks, stones, desert plants, and broken glass, scattered about. Traveling with Cooney was McLerran's eighty-year-old Aunt Frances. She too, had been one of the Roxaboxen children. With her help, Cooney was able to capture the spirit of this very special place.

Many Different Directions

⭐ **Locate Arizona on a map.** Point out Phoenix, Tucson, Scottsdale, and the Mexican border. Trace the Colorado River. Call attention to the Grand Canyon, and the Indian reservations. Find Yuma. Recall that this was the setting for the story. Talk about the sand, the rocks, the plants, the desert colors. With the group, see what else you can learn about this state... and the desert. Set up a display.

⭐ **Have a "Treasure" Hunt.** Search for treasures hidden in this story. Skim the book to find plants, animals, and other signs of desert life. See how many interesting details children can discover. Post this information on a chart.

Think about "places to play." Make a list of places kids like to play. From yards... to parks... to basements... to treehouses, there are lots of possibilites. As a story connection, have youngsters interview parents and/or grandparents to find out about places where they use to play. Add these to this list.

THE DESERT

Plants Animals Sights

Make travel folders for *Roxaboxen.* Since this is a place that should appeal to children of all ages, suggest that youngsters create advertisements/brochures for the town of Roxaboxen. Have them write copy and draw pictures that tell about this place in Yuma, Arizona. Encourage students to use words and pictures to "persuade" readers to visit this place.

Set up a bakery... or an ice cream parlor. Create your own play center. Recall that the children in Roxaboxen had a bakery and two ice cream parlors. Use that information as a springboard for a class project. Youngsters can cast votes for the kind of store they feel would be the most fun. Then, the group can use their imaginations, and available resources, to set up a new place to play. Help children layout a plan, and determine what is needed.

Read *The Salamander Room* by Anne Mazer aloud (Random House, 1994), another story that shows the magic of a child's imagination.

Today's Flavors
- Coconut
- Almond
- Cherry
- Maple

SPRINKLES 15¢

Cones

Nuts   Sodas

Name_____

Roxaboxen

The children of *Roxaboxen* had fun using their imaginations.
So can you. Remember what they did. Tell what you would do.

In *Roxaboxen*	In my neighborhood
what the kids used for a horse	what I would use for a horse
what the kids used for a car	what I would use for a car
what the kids used to make a house	what I would use for a house
what the kids used for furniture	what I would use for furniture

Teacher's Note: This activity enables youngsters to think about imaginary places and things.

Name_____

Roxaboxen

Make a Peek-a-book Box!
Put some little rocks... into an empty box.
Show a part of Roxaboxen.

You'll need: an empty shoe box with a lid, modeling clay (for the little rocks), colored paper, tin foil, pipe cleaners, glue, scissors

Directions
- Cut out a square window in the middle of the box top
- Cover the top with tin foil. Make sure the window is open.
- Then, cover the box with tin foil.
- Line the bottom of the box with paper.
- Set up a scene from Roxaboxen.
- Roll the clay to make little rocks.
- Bend pipe cleaners.
- Cut shapes out of colorful paper.
- Add one or two signs.
- Put the top on the box.
- Look inside your Peek-a -Book box! Invite others to peek inside, too.

The House I Live In

by Isadore Seltzer
Scholastic, 1992

From an adobe home in New Mexico... to an old stone house in Pennsylvania... to a colorful Victorian in San Francisco... to a log cabin in Montana, taking a look at houses is a great way to see this country. As the book moves from house to house, the reader gets a bit of history, geography, and sociology. Seeing where people live— and how they live— is an interesting way to open up some new doors.

Behind The Scenes

Since this house tour begins with a seven hundred year old adobe home in New Mexico, I decided to place this book in the southwest region. However, this book presents homes scattered all over the country, and therefore, can be used in any number of ways. Not only does this book enhance the regional theme, it offers another way to learn about places around the U.S. *The House I Live In* is packed with information about our country's past and the people who settled here. The book explains how homes were built... where they were built... and why each kind of home was built. Children of all ages should appreciate the stories behind these houses... and enjoy learning about different building materials and tools.

Many Different Directions

Go on a "House Hunt." Compile a list of the different kinds of houses introduced in *The House I Live In.* Find pictures of these houses in old magazines and newspapers. Label them and put them on display. Learn about other houses built in this country. Collect pictures of a colonial, a Cape Cod, a saltbox, etc. Before each home is posted on the bulletin board, help children choose a label for it.

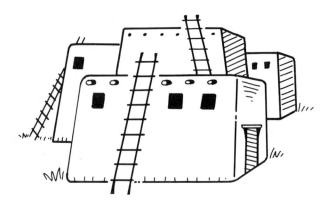

★ **Create your own "The House I Live In" booklet.** Children can draw pictures of their own homes, along with a descriptive sentence or two, and contribute to this class book.

★ **Plan an "Open House."** Create model houses from the book. Show children how to fold a piece of drawing paper, so that it opens like a house. Cut the top of the house in the shape of the roof. Decorate the outside of the house. Then, open the front doors... and design the inside.

how to fold the paper

how to shape the roof

the finished product

★ **Write a "how to."** Recall story details on building a log cabin. Go over the building process, step by step. Then, write easy- to-follow directions.

★ **Learn about houses in your neighborhood/community.** Read classified ads. Discover that there are many different kinds of houses for sale. Encourage children to make their own observations about homes in your area.

★ **Set up an "In the Home" display.** Gather different kinds of materials that are used in building. Show basic resources such as mud, twigs, stones, and sand. Bring in one or two bricks, a small piece of sanded wood, and pictures of a variety of building materials and tools. Use book details to determine some of the things people think about when building a house. Discuss the ways that each of these factors is important—

• the weather
• the available resources
• the land, and the actual space available
• the builder's knowledge, experience, and skills

Name_____

The House I Live In

Look at the many places you went to on this house tour in a book.
Keep a record. Name each house you saw.
Tell where you saw it.
Remember something special about each house. Make notes.

The House	Where it was	My Notes
_____	_____	_____
_____	_____	_____
_____	_____	_____
_____	_____	_____
_____	_____	_____
_____	_____	_____
_____	_____	_____
_____	_____	_____
_____	_____	_____

Teacher's Notes: This visual aid will help youngsters recall book details, and share them with family members. This record-keeping activity can also be used in conjunction with a map of the country. Children can place house markers all over a blank map to create another visual aid— a story map to accompany this book.

Name_____

The House I Live In

People of all ages build houses... even children.
They can build treehouses.

You might build a treehouse.
First you must make some decisions. Think about...
• the size of the treehouse
• the shape of the treehouse
• the style of the treehouse
• the building materials for the treehouse
• the location of your treehouse (Which tree?)

Jot down your ideas.

To make a treehouse unique, you need a good plan... and lots of imagination. Picture the kind of house you would build.
Make a sketch below.

Teacher's Note: Thinking about available resources, and the whole process of building something enables youngsters to get some hands-on experience.

Mountain

DID YOU KNOW?

▶ That Nevada means "snow-covered"...

▶ That Yellowstone National Park, which covers parts of Wyoming, Montana, and Idaho, is the world's oldest national park...

▶ That Mesa Verde, Colorado, has the best-preserved prehistoric cliff-dwellings in the United States

▶ That the Grand Teton mountains of Wyoming are the winter feeding grounds of the largest elk herd in America...

▶ That there is a city in Utah named Deseret, which means "land of honeybees," according to the Book of Mormon...

The Legend of the Indian Paintbrush

by Tomie dePaola
Scholastic, 1988

Long ago, a little boy named Gopher lived on the Great Plains. Although he always tried to keep up with the other boys in the tribe, he just couldn't.

Since he was not destined to be a warrior, Gopher had to find his own special place among his people. His talents as an artist enabled him to appreciate available resources and to see the beauty of colors... sunsets... and his environment.

Behind The Scenes

Tomie dePaola has been always been interested in folktales. No matter what their ethnic origin, he believes that folktales teach us about life... and people. The "Author's Note" at the end of this story explains how he got the idea for the Indian Paintbrush story. It also mentions *The Legend of the Blue Bonnet*, his tale about the state flower of Texas.

Since the Indian Paintbrush is the state flower of Wyoming, and the author dedicates this book to his friends who shared their part of Wyoming with him, this selection is in the Rocky Mountain section.

However, spectacular fields of Indian Paintbrush do bloom in Texas, too. Why not use this story, along with *The Legend of the Blue Bonnet*, to learn more about Texas and the southwest.

Many Different Directions

Locate Wyoming on a map. Point out the Great Plains— that narrow strip located along the eastern border of the state. Explain that this is part of a huge plain area that extends from Canada to Mexico. With the group, gather books and information about the Great Plains. See what you can learn.

WYOMING

cheyenne ★

⭐ **Experiment with paint... and paintbrush.** Provide paper, watercolors, and easel paintbrushes(large, fat brushes). Tell children to dip the large brush into the paint, and dab it on paper. (The brush would be used like a sponge in sponge painting.) Using this technique, youngsters can create their own pictures of the Indian Paintbrush flowers.

⭐ **Point out the close relationship between Native Americans and nature.** Recall story details that show how Little Gopher appreciates and respects the land, the natural resources, and the sunsets. Determine why it's important for everyone to care for the environment. List things that your students and their families do to show their concern.

⭐ **Try rock painting.** Mention that Little Gopher liked to decorate smooth stones with berry juice. Plan a similar project. First, go on a rock hunt. Ask each child to find a rock/shape that they like. Rinse the rocks with water. Dry them thoroughly with paper towels. Then, display magic markers in a variety of colors. Suggest that youngsters use their imaginations... and decorate the rocks. Put together your own rock collection.

⭐ **Make up some new color words.** Ask children to think of original names for colors they'd like to use. Suggest "sky blue," "red rose," "grass green," and other colors from nature. On a bulletin board, set up a colorful paintbrush display. Post the names on these paper paintbrushes.

⭐ **Read aloud** *The Legend of the Blue Bonnet*, Tomie dePaola's book about the state flower of Texas. Use this story as a springboard for learning more about this state, its major cities, and places of interest.

THE Colors of Nature

Sunny Yellow

Star White

Fern Green

Rose Red

Storm Gray

Name_____

The Legend of the Indian Paintbrush

Make a teepee. You will need: scissors, crayons, a stapler.
Draw pictures on the teepee. Cut it out along the solid lines.
Move the solid line to the dotted line, matching the X's, and staple together.
Tell about great deeds.

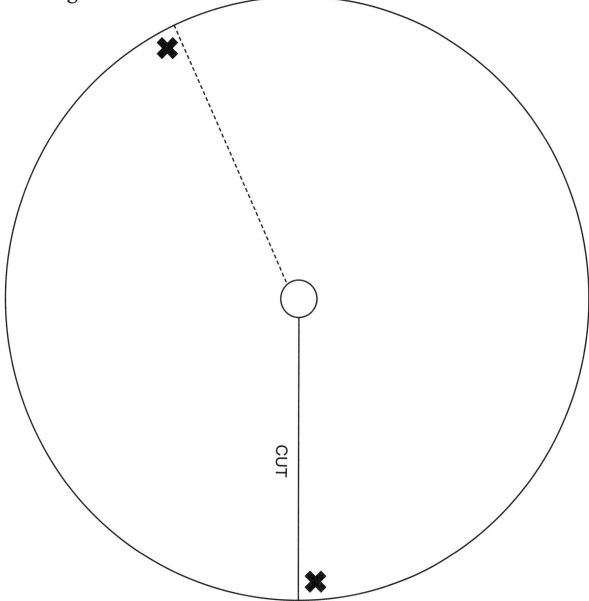

CUT

Teacher's Note: As a group, the children can recreate the setting from the story. On a display table, have them set up a circle of teepees.

Name_____

The Legend of the Indian Paintbrush

Remember all the things Little Gopher used to make his art. Think of some things that you could use. Share your ideas.

	What Little Gopher Used	What I Would Use
to make paints		
to make brushes		
to paint pictures on		
to make toys		

Teacher's Note: Use this activity to help children think about and appreciate available resources.

All the Places To Love

by Patricia MacLachlan
HarperCollins, 1994

The valley... the river... the hilltop... the barn... the meadows... the hay fields... every member of this family has a favorite spot. *All the Places to Love* is a tribute to the American farm... and to family and roots.The story captures the sights, the sounds, and the beauty of a place that is in the hearts of the grandparents... the parents... and the children.

Behind The Scenes

Patricia MacLachlan was born in Cheyenne, Wyoming, and now lives in Massachusetts. The author loves to travel— especially to the west and through the plains. MacLachlan says that every now and then, she must see and touch the prairie. This writer doesn't write about a place, unless she's been there and knows all about it— - how the land looks, the colors of the sky, etc. This story takes us to a place that she knows very well. Her family farm is filled with all kinds of places to see and appreciate.

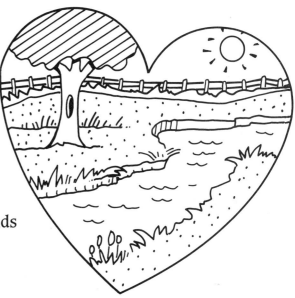

Many Different Directions

Locate Wyoming on a map. Find Cheyenne, MacLachlan's birthplace. Note that this is the state capital. Since Wyoming has many places that will appeal to children, compile a list of "All the Places to... see." Browse through books and travel brochures.

Create an *"All the Places to Love"* scrapbook. Identify the favorite place of each story character. Remember that grandfather loved the barn; grandmother loved the river; Eli loved the marsh; etc. Make pictures and write simple descriptions of each of these places. Assemble them in a class-made version of a family album.

⭐ **"Name" etchings.** Recall that the grandfather carved names on a rafter in the barn. Think of other places where people might carve names. Then, have each child create a colorful place to carve his/her name. Plan to do crayon etchings. Have youngsters cover a whole sheet of paper with crayon designs. Then, using a black crayon, have them color over that entire page. Children can carve their own names— and those of family members— using a pencil point, or the tip of a paper clip.

⭐ **Write a "How To."** Explain how to make a bark boat. Talk about the boat that the grandmother made. Name the different materials that she used. Tell where she sailed these boats and how she used them to send messages. Then, write simple step by step directions.

⭐ **Make a story map.** With the group, take an imaginary tour of the farm. Remember all the places described in this story— the barn, the river, the hay fields, the hilltop, etc. Show "all the places to love" on a large chart. Make a visual aid to go along with the story.

⭐ **Visit a local farm.** If possible, plan a trip to a farm nearby. As children tour the place, they can enjoy the sights, the sounds, the smells, and the colors. After the trip, put together a memory book. Each child can contribute some descriptions and/or pictures of their favorite spots.

Name_____

All the Places to Love

Grandmother made boats with messages. You can, too.

Make this boat for someone in your family.
Cut along the solid lines. Fold along the dotted lines.
Tape the sides together.
Put a special message on the boat.

Name_____

All the Places to Know

Think about all the places to love... on the farm.

the barn   the hay fields   the river   the marsh

Remember that there were many sights to see.

Think about what you read. Think about what you saw.

Name some things you remember. Write them on the chart below.

On the Farm

the animals	
the birds	
the fish	
the plants	

Teacher's Note: Completing this chart will call attention to the many things that live on a farm.

Pacific

Alaska

Washington

Oregon

Hawaii

California

DID YOU KNOW?

▶ that you can see active volcanoes in this part of the country...

▶ that Crater Lake in Oregon is the deepest lake in the country...

▶ that Mt. McKinley, in Alaska, is the highest peak in all of North America...

▶ that there's a place called *Death Valley,* in the California desert...

▶ that some tropical fish in Hawaii can not be seen anyplace else in the world...

Grandfather's Journey

by Allen Say
Houghton Mifflin, 1993

This 1994 Caldecott winner tells of a grandfather who leaves his home in Japan so that he can see more of the world. His journey begins on a steamship, and takes him to a new land. After touring America, grandfather settles in California— the place he loves most. However, he never stops missing Japan. Yet, when he returns to Japan, there is much he misses about California.

Behind The Scenes

Allen Say was born in Yokohama, Japan, and came to the United States when he was sixteen years old. He now lives in San Francisco, California. The idea of loving two countries is apparently something he understands well.

In this cross-cultural account, Say shows us how it is for someone to feel torn between two places. Through his grandfather's eyes, he shows the beauty and diversity of America... <u>and</u> his homeland. This touching story contains beautiful paintings, wonderful scenery, and lots of new learning experiences.

Many Different Directions

★ **Locate Japan on a globe.** Determine that this was the grandfather's homeland. Point out the Pacific Ocean. Then, trace the route grandfather must have taken when he set sail for the "New World." Help children visualize the trip across the ocean and identify the part of the U.S. where he first landed.

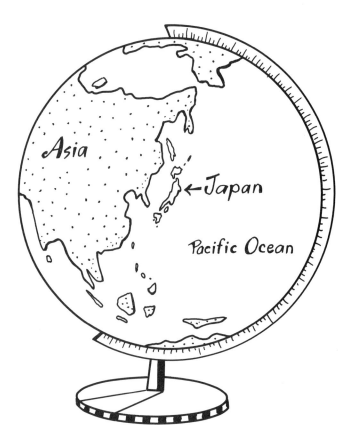

100

⭐ **Create a "Grandfather's Journey" interactive chart.** Make the word *journey* replaceable. Place blank cards near the chart so that children can think of other words/phrases that tell about this story. See how many possibilities students think of.

⭐ **Paint scenery.** Study and appreciate all the paintings in this story. Talk about the colors, the shapes, and the details in the desert, farm fields, city scenes, etc. Set up an easel— with paper, watercolors, and brushes. Invite individual students to visit the art center and paint a favorite scene from the story. Fill the room with colorful sights.

⭐ **Discover interesting ways to travel.** Name the different modes of transportation that Grandfather used, to get from place to place. Begin a list including— *steamship*, *train*, *riverboat*, and *on foot*. See how many other possiblities children can think of. Add them to the list.

⭐ **Locate California on a map.** Recall that after traveling around the country, grandfather made his home by the San Francisco Bay. Point out the bay and San Francisco. With the group, gather books, travel brochures, and information about this city and its attractions. Be sure to talk about the cable cars— another way to travel around and see the sights.

⭐ **Interview grandparents.** Ask about a place of birth... a childhood home... and/or a place to remember always. Have children write a few sentences about what they learn. Share them with classmates.

Name_____

Grandfather's Journey Name Game

Play a Name Game. Think of the *first* letter of your *first* name.
Write that letter in the box below.

Look at each category below. Think of something that begins with the same
letter as the one in the box. See how many things you can name.

★ a state_____

★ a capital_____

★ a river_____

★ a lake_____

★ a famous building_____

★ a natural resource_____

★ a tourist attraction_____

★ a place near your home_____

★ a state's nickname_____

Give 1 point for each correct answer.
What was your total score? _____

Play this game again. This time, use the *first* letter... of your *last* name!

Name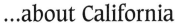

Grandfather's Journey

Grandfather traveled everywhere.
But he loved two places best.

Draw what grandfather liked best...

...about California	...about Japan

	In California	In Japan
What Grandfather did...		
How Grandfather dressed...		
How Grandfather felt...		

Teacher's Note: Extend this activity by having youngsters talk to their own grandparents or senior citizens they know about places that they love.

Alaska's Three Bears

by Shelly Gill
Paws IV Publishing, 1990

In this unique version of the "Three Bears", there's much to learn about the Grizzly Bear, the Polar Bear, the Black Bear, and Alaska. The clever story, along with the "bear" facts at the bottom of each page, provide a great view of the land and the wildlife. This is a nice way to get a glimpse of bear country and to see how fact and fiction can be used together.

Behind The Scenes

Shannon Cartwright and Shelly Gill have created a number of children's books about Alaska. Both woman live there, and are considered authorities on that part of our country.

On January 3, 1959, Alaska became the forty-ninth state. In addition to being our largest state, it's also one of the most interesting. The climate, the mountain ranges, the wilderness, the glaciers, the volcanoes, and the Eskimos— are just a few of the topics that children will want to explore.

Many Different Directions

⭐ **Locate Alaska on a map.** Name the bodies of water that surround this state. Point out the Aleutian Islands and Kodiak Island. Note the size of Alaska, in relation to the other states. Note its location, in relation to the other states. Find out more about this state and what makes it unique. Display books, travels brochures, and information about Alaska. Have children share what they learn.

⭐ **Write your own "Bear" facts.** Include information on all three bears. Use book details to describe their size... their appearance... what they eat... how they move... etc. See how much information you can put under each heading.

Polar Bear	Grizzly Bear	Black Bear
has light fur	eats meat	smallest of the three

★ **Read maps.** Study the three simple maps depicted on the first two pages of this story. Help children determine what each map tells about each bear. Identify the places where each bear can be found. Decide if any of the bears can be seen... where you live.

★ **Go on an "animal" hunt.** Learn about other animals that are found in the wilderness. Skim the story to find the animals mentioned. Make a list. Ask interested volunteers to gather facts about other animals that live in Alaska. Have them share this information with the class.

arctic fox

ringed seal

★ **Talk about animal adaptations.** Call attention to the special qualities that enable bears to survive. Reread the information about the polar bear's hair, being transluscent, not white. Explain that if the bear's hair were really white, it would reflect the sun's rays and heat, and might cause the bear to freeze from the cold. Besides keeping warm, determine why else polar bears have hair that appears white.

★ **Read aloud *Kiana's Iditarod* (Paws IV Publishing, 1984), another Alaskan adventure by Shelley Gill and Shannon Cartwright.** The Iditarod, a thousand mile dog sled trip from Anchorage to Nome, is a world famous race that takes place annually. This picture book captures the spirit of that race... the beauty of Alaska... and the struggles and hardships of the wilderness.

polar bear

Name_____

Alaska's Three Bears

Show how big the three bears are. Make a bar graph.
Use a yellow crayon... a brown crayon... and a black crayon.

8-10 feet	6-8 feet	5-6 feet
the big	the medium-sized	the small
white bear	brown bear	black bear

feet

The Three Bears

feet			
10			
8			
6			
4			
2			
	Black Bears	Grizzly Bears	Polar Bears

Teacher's Note: By showing this information on the bar graph, youngsters can actually see how these bears compare in size.

Name_____

Alaska's Three Bears

Write about bears.
Choose one of the activities below.
Write on the bottom of this paper.

❑ **Make up your own story about "The Three Bears."** Begin with "Once upon a time, there were three bears... "

❑ **What do you think? Read the paragraph below and give your opinion.**

❑ **Which bear from the story was your favorite? Tell some things you learned about that bear.**

❑ **Pretend you will take a trip to bear country. What should you know about bears? Write some safety rules.**

_____

_____

_____

_____

Anno's U.S.A.

Mitsumasa Anno
Philomel, 1983

In this wordless book, a lone traveler approaches this country on the west coast... and makes his journey eastward. Since this country was originally settled from east to west, going in the opposite direction is a unique way to explore and share some of its history. There is so much to see and do, that the book can be enjoyed again and again. Plus, this overview of the country helps bring this "read across America" theme to an end.

Behind The Scenes

Mitsumasa Anno was born and raised in Tsuwano, Japan. Even as a young child, Anno wanted to know more about the world beyond his village. His first trip to Europe inspired him to write the book *Anno's Journey.* On that trip, he wanted to see more of the the world. But, more than that, he wanted to lose himself in it. That kind of thinking was the beginning of a series of books, based on Anno's travels.

A lone horseman travels through all of Anno's journey books. He represents the spirit of exploring and making discoveries, a spirit that Anno loves to share with his readers. This artist actually hides all kinds of surprises within his drawings. Finding those pictures of well-known storybook characters or famous paintings allows readers to explore, make discoveries, and go on a unique kind of treasure hunt.

For additional information about the author/illustrator and this book, read the Afterword in *Anno's U.S.A.*

Many Different Directions

⭐ **Plan your own journey.** With small groups, explore the pages of this book, and make your own discoveries. Refer to the map as you travel. Whenever possible, provide interesting bits of history, geography, music, art, and literature. Also, point out familiar sights from some of the other stories in this program.

⭐ **Enjoy the scenery in Central Park in Anno's book.** Examine this New York City landmark and talk about the statues(especially the one of the lone traveler)... the people... and the various activities. Compile a list of the things people do in this park. Then, plan a fun activity of your own. Look through the trees. Turn this picture in all different directions. See how many zoo animals you can find hidden there.

Appreciate familiar sights. Remember the Old State House in Boston... and Robert McCloskey's *Make Way for Ducklings* (worth searching for). See them again, in *Anno's U.S.A.* Skim through the book to find the Alamo, the Capitol Building in Washington, Independence Hall in Philadelphia, and sights children will recognize from some of the other stories they've read.

Study architecture. From log cabins, to adobe homes, to stone houses, to one room schoolhouses, to landmark buildings and churches, children can see all kinds of structures and make some interesting observations. Why not ask each child to sketch a favorite building from the book. Follow up by having them write something about that place. (As you skim through this book, don't forget to point out homes described in Isadore Seltzer's *The House I Live In.*)

Make your own _____'s U.S.A. wordless books. Children can use their own names, in place of *Anno's*. To make each booklet, staple together six to eight pages of construction paper. As a culminating project, youngsters can share their own views of different parts of this country. Using a combination of available resources— magazine pictures, newspaper photos, sketches, travel folders — children can create collages to tell a story of this country.

Plan a book talk. Compare and contrast *Anno's U.S.A* and *Grandfather's Journey* by Allen Say. Decide how these books are similar... and how they are different.

Learn about Hawaii. Examine the introductory picture of the traveler approaching the West Coast. Notice that little island with the swimmers, surfers, dancers, musician, and pineapples. Anno has given kids a peek at another place to explore. Use the globe to help them determine that this represents Hawaii. Then, display books, pictures, and travel brochures to see what they can find out about this place.

Write words for Anno's wordless book. As an ongoing project, write simple text for the pictures in this book. Because there is so much to see, discover, and explore, the possibilities are endless. Whether children work alone, in pairs, or, in small groups, each time they study a picture, they'll probably see something they didn't see before.

Name_____

Anno's U.S.A.

Remember what you saw as you traveled through Anno's book. Think about a place you've traveled to or heard about.

A place I remember _____

Where it's located _____

What I know about that place_____

_____

What I'd like to find out _____

_____

_____

Show what it looks like. Make a sketch.

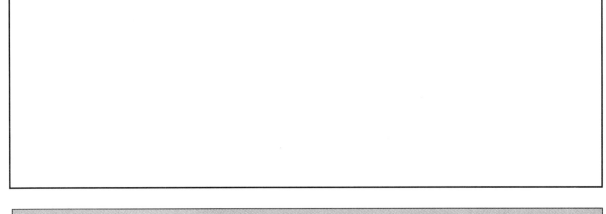

Teacher's Note: Use this activity to help children appreciate how Anno's book takes them on a trip.

Name_____

Anno's U.S.A.

Go on a "treasure" hunt.
Learn more about the U.S.A.
Look through the pictures in this book.
See if you can find...

I Found

❏ a well-known storybook character

❏ a symbol of our country

❏ a popular sport

❏ a symbol of a holiday

❏ an unexpected surprise

Teacher's Note: Since there are lots of unexpected treasures in this book, children can make some of their own discoveries. There can be many 'right' answers.

Resources

New England

Harwood, Lynne. *Honeybees at Home* (Tilbury House, 1994)

Kinsey-Warnock, Natalie and Helen Kinsey. *The Bear that Heard Crying* (Dutton, 1993)

Krupinski, Loretta. *New England Scrapbook: A Journey Through Poems, Prose, and Pictures* (HarperCollins, 1994)

Weller, Frances W. *I Wonder if I'll See a Whale* (Putnam, 1995)

Wells, Rosemary. *Waiting for the Evening Star* (Dial, 1993)

Middle Atlantic

Ammon, Richard. *Growing Up Amish* (Macmillan, 1989)

Khalsa, Dayal Kaur. *How Pizza Came to Queens* (Crown, 1989)

Moutran, Julia S. *The Story of Punxsutawney Phil, "The Fearless Forecaster"* (Avon, 1987)

Southeast

Donnelley, Judy. *A Wall of Names: The Story of the Vietnam Vererans Memorial* (Random House, 1991)

Houston, Gloria M. *My Great-Aunt Arizona* (HarperCollins, 1992)

Isaacs, Anne. *Swamp Angel* (Dutton, 1994)

Mills, Lauren. *The Rag Coat* (Little, Brown, 1991)

Pedersen, Anne. *Kidding Around Washington, D.C.: A Young Person's Guide* (John Muir Publications, 1993)

Midwest

Edwards, Michelle. *Eve and Smithy: An Iowa Tale* (LL&S, 1995)

Eitzen, Ruth. *The White Feather* (Herald Press, 1987)

Henry, Joanne L *Log Cabin in the Woods: A True Story About a Pioneer Boy* (Four Winds, 1988)

Okimoto, Jean D. *Blumpoe the Grumpoe Meets Arnold the Cat* (Little, Brown, 1990)

Southwest

Cherry, Lynne. *The Armadillo from Amarillo* (Harcourt, Brace, 1994)

Cobb, Vicki. *This Place is Dry* (Walker, 1989)

Harper, Jo. *Jalapeno Hal* (Macmillan, 1993)

Johnston, Tony *Alice Nizzy Nazzy, the Witch of Santa Fe* IPutnam, 1995)

Keegan, Marcia *Pueblo Boy: Growing up in Two Worlds* (Dutton, 1991)

Mountain

Arnold, Caroline. *Dinosaur Mountain* (Ticknor and Fields, 1990)

Horner, John R. and Don Lessen. *Digging up Tyrannosaurus Rex* (Crown, 1995)

Johnson, Neil. *Jack Creek Cowboy* (Dial, 1993)

Lucas, Barbara M. *Snowed In* (Macmillan, 1993)

Siebert, Diane. *Sierra* (Harpercollins, 1991)

Pacific

Bunting, Eve. *Smoky Night* (Harcourt, Brace, 1994)

London, Jonathan. *Condor's Egg* (Chronicle Books, 1994)

Love, D. Anne. *Bess's Log Cabin Quilt* (Holiday House, 1995)

McDermott, Gerald *Raven: A Trickster Tale from the Pacific Northwest* (Harcourt, Brace, 1993)